When the Loving Stopped

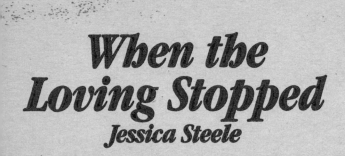

Jessica Steele

Harlequin Books

TORONTO • NEW YORK • LONDON
AMSTERDAM • PARIS • SYDNEY • HAMBURG
STOCKHOLM • ATHENS • TOKYO • MILAN

Original hardcover edition published in 1988
by Mills & Boon Limited

ISBN 0-373-02982-9

Harlequin Romance first edition May 1989

CHAPTER ONE

LIFE had been a shade dull of late. Having left the party to seek refuge in the cloakroom, Whitney considered that maybe she was happy with her dull existence. She wasn't enjoying this particular party, that was for sure. She wished, not for the first time that evening, that she had not given in to Toby Keston's plea that she partner him at the event.

'Do come,' he'd begged earnestly. 'I know you told me you were "off" men when I asked you for a date a couple of weeks ago, but I wouldn't be a nuisance. Honestly, I wouldn't.'

Toby worked for the same firm and, like herself, was twenty-three years of age, but to Whitney he seemed years younger. She liked him quite well, but only because there was simply nothing in the eager-to-please junior executive that anyone could possibly dislike.

'Oh, please come,' Toby had renewed his persuasions, and had made a gaping hole in Whitney's defences when, looking like a little boy lost, he'd said in scared tones, 'Val's threatened to partner me with a female from her worldly-wise set if I can't bring my own partner!'

Whitney wasn't so certain about the implication that she herself could not be from the 'worldly-wise' set, but she relented and put Toby out of his misery. 'So, I'll come,' she told him. 'Which part of London does your sister live in?' she asked, and realised that she was committed to go with him when, his relief evident, he replied cheerfully,

'Oh, the party's not at Val's place!'

'It isn't?'

He shook his head, and was still cheerful as he revealed that it was something in the nature of a surprise party for the fiancé of one of his sister's girlfriends. Apparently, Whitney gleaned, someone by the name of Gleda Caufield was engaged to some globe-trotting industrialist who was returning to England after a three-month absence. Gleda, with Valerie's help, was drumming up everyone they could think of to give him a resounding 'welcome home'.

'He'll—er—like that, will he?' Whitney asked; to her way of thinking, any man who had been away for three months could be forgiven for preferring to have his fiancée solely to himself. Still, perhaps this was the natural way to go on in the 'worldly-wise' set.

'Gleda seems to think so, and so does Valerie,' Toby replied. 'And, since Gleda has the full co-operation of the housekeeper at Heathlands...'

'Heathlands?' Whitney queried.

'Sloan Illingworth's home in Berkshire,' Toby promptly supplied.

The name of her unsuspecting host passed Whitney by just then. 'Berkshire!' she exclaimed.

'It's no distance at all via the motorway,' Toby assured her, and added, 'Val has plenty of room in her car. She says she'll drive us, then I shan't have to watch how much I drink.'

Whitney had elected to wear a cool, loose-fitting dress with slender shoulder-straps on that warm May evening when Toby Keston and his sister called for her. Any notion she might have had, though, that Valerie Keston must in some way resemble her younger brother was way off-beam. For not only were they the opposite in looks, but, where Toby was warm and sweet and kind, his sister came across as being cold and as hard as nails.

They had arrived at Heathlands without Whitney changing her opinion of Valerie Keston. 'Circulate,' she had instructed her brother, and with a synthetic cry of 'Darling!' she had waltzed up to a slightly corpulent man. Taking possession of his arm, she left Toby to find their hostess and to introduce Whitney.

'How lovely of you to come,' Gleda, an elegant, self-assured blonde, purred at Whitney and, using her left hand, on which was displayed a magnificent and colossally expensive-looking sapphire and diamond engagement ring, she waved in the general direction of where everyone appeared to be helping themselves to drinks, and turned to someone else. 'Darling, how lovely of you to come,' Whitney heard her repeat.

'How lovely of you to come!' Whitney made a face at her reflection in the cloakroom mirror. It seemed a lifetime away since she had first heard Gleda Caufield murmur her phoney welcome, yet it was only three hours ago.

Wishing that the globe-trotting industrialist would soon make his appearance so that she could make noises about going home, Whitney, with her innate good manners, suddenly remembered that she couldn't stay skulking in the cloakroom for evermore.

Someone else coming into the small ante-room saw Whitney touching her fingers to her long, dark brown hair as if she had just been tidying it. Trying to put something of a smile into her large green eyes, she then nodded to the newcomer and went back to join a party which had deteriorated in no time into a glorified 'booze-up'.

The main body of the party, she discovered, had moved in the time she had been away, and now seemed to be concentrated in what had previously appeared to be an enormous hall.

She could see no sign of Toby, though, so she guessed that he was most likely still in the drawing-room. With the intention of going to find him—even though he had seemed very near plastered the last time she had spoken to him—she side-stepped a lurching, bottle-carrying reveller and grew irritated that everyone there seemed to think that the only way to have a good time was to get smashed out of one's skull.

'I've got one somewhere,' she said as pleasantly as she was able, when the lurching man extended his shaky hold on the bottle in her general direction.

'Be like that, toffee-nose,' he slurred, offended, and went lurching on his way.

It was then that Whitney discovered the marathon task she had set herself in going to look for Toby. Five minutes later she was still trying to make her way through the mass of bodies that gyrated to music coming from a tape deck somewhere.

She was wasting her time showing her annoyance when males who were the worse for drink tried to grab hold of her, for they were past caring. Her annoyance went beyond the bounds of just plain irritation though when, espying a gap and making for it, she was grabbed from behind by a red-faced, sweaty-looking individual.

'Come on, sweetie,' he leered, 'let's dance,' and before she could get away from him he placed his clammy hands on her bare shoulders, making her feel downright ill. Careless of whom they cannoned into, he had whirled her round a couple of times before, giving him something else to put his clammy hands on, she managed to dig her elbow into his solar plexus.

She heard him grunt, and she was free. Whitney did not wait around to apologise, but went swiftly ahead.

She barged her way angrily through the dancers, halting when, having gone round a bend, she found that she at last had some space, and that she had come to the bottom of the staircase. She forgot about the staircase momentarily, though, when she became aware that her successful attempt to get away from the clammy-handed man had not been without casualty, and that the back part of the slender strap over the right shoulder of her dress had been wrenched from its moorings. She was cross enough to wish that she had dug her elbow deeper into the man's podgy flesh, but then she forgot about him for a moment when, to her surprise, she noticed that access to the staircase had been blocked off by a series of gates and hurdles.

Wondering, for all the housekeeper was said to have co-operated over the party, if she was concerned to keep the party isolated to the ground floor, Whitney turned her back on the staircase. Whoever had had the brainwave to gate the stairs, it had been successful, for she could imagine but few of those assembled still being firm-footed enough to climb to reach the out-of-bounds area, even if they thought of doing so.

Tucking her broken shoulder-strap inside the top of her dress, Whitney took a few steps and peered round the bend to see that the party was still in full swing. In the hope of spotting Toby, she took a quick scan of the people there. The one face she spotted above all others, however, was that of the red-faced clown whose clammy hands had been responsible for her broken shoulder-strap.

'Oh, bother it,' she muttered crossly between her teeth, for it was obvious that he was searching for someone. Seeing herself as the most likely candidate, Whitney ducked back around the corner, and saw that her only escape lay in an upward direction.

Not wanting to feel those clammy hands on her again, she lightly but firm-footedly set about going where she had every faith that that man could not go.

Having reached the first-floor landing, she stood back in the shadows where the light from the bottom of the stairs could not penetrate. It was from there that she reviewed the situation.

Apart from her feeling of revulsion at the thought of having that man's hands on her again, she supposed he was otherwise quite harmless. But it went without saying that he could well prove tedious if she met up with him again and, from her point of view, she'd had her share of tedium for the evening.

Realising that she preferred her own company to that of any of the people downstairs—and, since Toby had looked slightly the worse for drink the last time she had seen him, that included him—Whitney stayed where she was. Relaxing her slender frame against a wall, she heartily wished that Sloan Illingworth, or whatever his name was, would hurry up and soon come home.

How long she stood there, kicking against the knowledge that until their unsuspecting host arrived home she could not leave the party, Whitney could not have said. All she knew for sure just then was that, since Heathlands appeared to be in a very isolated area, and since she had no transport of her own, she was stuck at the party until Toby's sister wanted to leave.

Knowing without having to ask that Valerie Keston would think she had gone out of her mind if she asked her if she was ready to go yet, Whitney yawned from a mixture of tiredness and boredom. It was way past her normal bedtime.

Thinking of bedtime caused her to yearn for her bed, and she cast a look of longing at the bedroom door opposite where she stood. If nothing else, there would be somewhere quiet to sit in there, she considered. It took some effort of will to resist the impulse to go over and to try the door-handle, but Whitney did so, remembering that, since the housekeeper had seen fit to lock one or two of the downstairs rooms, she had probably locked all bedroom doors too.

When her good manners again decreed that she should not stay hiding away upstairs until the cry of 'Surprise, surprise!' went up, Whitney left her position by the wall. She sighed as, with the intention of joining the mêlée, she reluctantly crossed the landing.

Suddenly, though, and without her known volition, it seemed, she found that her hand was curled round the cold ceramic of the knob to the bedroom door. What was more, her fingers seemed incapable of leaving that door-knob until she had tested it. Whitney did just that, and discovered that the door was not locked.

Slowly, the door opened, but when she peered in, she could make out little from what small light penetrated the room, save that there appeared to be one gigantic-sized bed in there.

Bed, she thought wistfully, and resisted a dreadful compulsion to enter the room and to spend a few quiet moments inside. All at once, however, a shriek of uproarious laughter rent the air and, warned that the party had grown wilder, Whitney acted entirely on instinct, and was suddenly aware that she had bolted inside the bedroom.

Deciding she would take a short breather, she left the bedroom door ajar and, thinking to take her ease for only a few moments, she went and sat on the edge of the bed.

She had no idea who normally used this bedroom, but it was not all that important. She would not be staying for more than a minute.

It was good, though, to sit here in the quiet darkness. Much too late, she realised that she should never have given in to Toby's persuasions to partner him. Weariness of the whole wretched evening washed over her as she likened the goings-on downstairs more to a rugger scrum than to any party she had been to before.

Without thinking, she eased off her shoes and brought her feet up on to the mattress as a fair-minded and fresh thought dropped into her head. Was it the party which was at fault, or was it her? Was she a killjoy, that she had been able to find no pleasure whatsoever in the goings-on at the party? Would she feel the way she was feeling now if it had been Dermot she had partnered, and not Toby?

Painfully, Whitney wondered whether she would have felt the way she did now about things before she had met Dermot. Dermot...

Her thoughts flew back to six months ago. She had been a secretary at Hobson's Garden Implements then, and had enjoyed her work. Then, one Monday, Dermot Selby had started work there as the new sales manager, and, as he was introduced around, he and Whitney had met.

From that first handshake, from his first 'I just know that I'm going to enjoy working here', Whitney had known that her life would never again be the same.

Nor was it. In no time she and Dermot were dating each other as regularly as Dermot could manage it. For, as he had explained, 'Were it not for my new job, and the fact that I've so much to learn, so much work to put in if I'm to be the best sales manager Hobson's has ever had, I'd see you every night of the week, my pet. But...'

'Don't say any more, I understand,' she had told him, grateful for the two evenings a week he could manage and wishing that she was his secretary so that she could work late with him. Quite simply, she loved him.

She had been going out with him for two months when, doing some bits of shopping one lunch hour, she had bumped into Amanda Clarke, the woman who *was* lucky enough to be Dermot's secretary. Since neither knew the other well, Whitney had made some pleasant remark in passing, and was about to go on when she saw Amanda hesitate. Whitney had hesitated, too, and that was how—the two of them halted—she had waited to hear what comment Amanda had to make. Only later had she realised that she had left Amanda with little choice but to say something.

What she did say, though, was to rock Whitney to her very foundations. 'Is it right, that you're going out with Dermot Selby?' she had asked in a sudden rush.

Suspecting that maybe Amanda was a tiny bit jealous, Whitney could none the less speak only the truth. 'Yes,' she had told her modestly, 'we've been going out together for some weeks now.'

Whitney had still been searching for words which might take the edge off any pain Amanda might be feeling when Amanda revealed that it was not jealousy which had made her hesitate and ask the question she had, but concern—concern for her! And it was not Amanda who felt pain, but Whitney, when Dermot

Selby's secretary said, 'You *do* know that—he's married, don't you?'

'*Married!*' Whitney had gasped, her exclamation revealing that she had known nothing of the sort. 'He can't be!' she'd further exclaimed. 'You've got it wrong! You've...'

'Ask him,' Amanda had cut in quietly, and she had walked away.

Reeling, not wanting to believe a word of it, Whitney had gone back to her office to have a fairly unproductive afternoon. He couldn't be married, went her thoughts. Perhaps he had been married, but was now divorced.

Had she not known that Dermot was out that afternoon, she might well have gone along to see him then to ask him outright. But, since he was not in his office that afternoon, Whitney had had to sweat it out until the evening. As luck would have it she'd had a date with him that night, but as the time for him to call at her flat had grown nearer she had been visited by a small memory or two. She had remembered the time she had bought a couple of theatre tickets to surprise Dermot over a show which he had expressed an interest in seeing.

'Would you believe it?' he'd groaned when she'd told him. 'I've a long-standing arrangement to—pick my aunt up from the airport on Saturday.'

Whitney had started to hate the logic which had suddenly woken up to ask, what up-and-coming thirty-year-old bachelor, who had never so much as mentioned having an aunt before, used up his Saturday nights in waiting for her at an airport? Did he, in fact, have an aunt who flew in occasionally, or—did his wife not let him out on Saturday nights?

WHEN THE LOVING STOPPED

She had felt sick inside at the thought, sick inside too as she recalled how, as she was hugging him goodbye one evening, Dermot must have thought that her mouth was much too close to his collar.

'Don't get lipstick on my shirt!' he had cried, alarmed.

'My, you are fastidious,' she had teased him, and had pointed out, 'I'm not wearing lipstick—now'.

Barely aware of what she was doing, Whitney moved from her sitting position on the over-large bed at Heathlands, and lay down. With her head against the pillows, she drew her knees up to her stomach as though to ward off more sickness, and her thoughts winged back to how she had opened the door to Dermot that Thursday night.

'Hello, pet,' he'd greeted her. 'What a sight you are for sore eyes!'

'Come in,' she had invited, but she hadn't been able to wait beyond climbing the stairs to her flat and closing the door after them before, backing away from the arms that would have grabbed her, she had asked him bluntly, 'Are you married?'

'What...? Who...? Don't be...'

His blustering evasion had hit at the gut of her. 'Goodbye, Dermot,' she had told him in frigid tones.

Ignoring his double-take at this new person he had not previously met, she had had the door open by the time he'd recovered to tell her, 'It's not what you think!'

'Are you or aren't you married?' she had persisted coldly, this new frigid-sounding person in charge of her a stranger to her, too—a stranger who had taken over from the normally quiet and unargumentative person she was more familiar with.

'I—am married. Yes, I'm married' Dermot had been forced to own. 'But I love *you*.'

She could feel herself weakening. She wanted Dermot to love her. That he should say he loved her was the fulfilment of all her dreams. 'But you still live with your wife?' she had asked, some of the ice leaving her voice, for, disappointed though she owned she was, perhaps she could adjust to him being a married man if he and his wife had decided to call it a day and were separated.

But the answer which Dermot had given her had not been the one she had been half-way to expecting. 'I have to live with her, for the moment,' he had replied.

'You—*have* to?'

'While the kids are small, I can do no other,' he had told her, shocking her into silence, because she just had not given a thought to the possibility that he might have children! 'But as soon as they're old enough, I'll be able to leave her, and you and I...'

But suddenly, Whitney was recovering from her shock. White-faced at what she had just learned, she had abruptly stopped him before he could go any further. 'You and I *nothing*!' she had told him, and, opening the door wide, she had refused to hear another word.

That night she had shed tears over a man who was just not worth her tears. When later she had dried her eyes, though, she'd wondered if those tears had all been on account of everything being over between her and Dermot, or if perhaps some of them had been because what had happened had resurrected the hurt of her mother's pain.

She had been twenty when, answering the door one day, she had been confronted by a woman of about thirty-five years of age. Whitney felt sick at heart when she thought of how, if only she had thought to ask the woman her business, she might have been able to save her mother from being utterly devastated. But they were a happy family unit, and she had seen nothing wrong in taking the woman through to the sitting-room when she had said that she would like to see Mrs Lawford.

"I'm sorry, I didn't get your name,' she remembered, smiling at the woman as she'd introduced her mother.

'My name's unimportant,' she had replied, and had then proceeded to render them both speechless when she had told them both that she was the mistress of Lawrence Lawford, and had been for the past five years. Shaken rigid as much by the length of time as by the fact that her father had a mistress, although at that stage she had not truly believed it, Whitney had been all set to show the woman the door. But just then Lawrence Lawford had arrived home, and as he entered the sitting-room three pairs of eyes were directed on him.

'What the...' he'd started to bluster, his eyes shooting from the woman who had just claimed to be his mistress to his ashen-faced wife.

'I had to come,' the woman had drawn his attention back to her, and while, horrified, Whitney had looked on, her father's mistress had revealed how he had promised and promised to leave his wife, but how she had finally got fed up with waiting, and had come to his home—perhaps in the hope of giving him a helping hand to tell his wife that he was leaving.

But it didn't turn out like that. For one thing, it had appeared that Lawrence Lawford had never had any intention of leaving his comfortable home. Nor did he. What had gone on between him and her mother afterwards, Whitney never knew, but her mother was never the same again. She grew vague, forgot to do things she said she would do, and Whitney had realised that, unable to get over the shock, her thoughts must constantly have been on her husband's betrayal.

Nor had she ever got over that betrayal. It must have been on her mind all the time, Whitney realised when, some months later, her mother, while out driving, with no one else involved, had crashed her car into a stationary lorry. She had never recovered from the motoring accident, and had died a few days later.

Whitney still loved her father, but she no longer felt close to him. When shortly afterwards he had married again—though not to the woman who had been his mistress—Whitney had left home.

She had gone to London, had lived in a hostel and had started work at Hobson's Garden Implements. She had been working at Hobson's for four months when she had been lucky in finding herself a flat.

The day after she had finished with Dermot Selby, Whitney gave in her notice at Hobson's. A month later she started work at Alford Plastics, and one of the first people she had met there was inoffensive Toby Keston.

'Are you doing anything tonight?' he had asked in the first week of her being there.

'Yes, I am!' she had told him belligerently, and had cared not a damn then whose feelings she hurt. A month later, though, and she was beginning to reason that not all men were the same. And the more she got to know Toby, the more she was able to see his vulnerability. Somehow, she just felt mean being nasty to him, and she ended up hurting no one but herself.

With thoughts of Toby back in her head, Whitney wondered if perhaps she ought to brave the party and go looking for him. However, she felt far more comfortable up here on her own than she had done since she had first set foot inside Heathlands. How many hours ago that was, she thought tiredly, the lord only knew. By her calculations—and it was too dark in the room to read the dial on her watch—Whitney guessed that it must be somewhere around two o'clock in the morning. And the racket was *still* going on downstairs!

More weariness crept over Whitney as she closed her eyes and tried to summon up the will to go and find Toby. The trouble was, it was so comfortable up here. Besides, if she didn't go down—with that uninhibited crew downstairs—she'd still be bound to hear the cheer that went up when the party-giver in chief arrived home.

Feeling a shade cold, she absently gathered some of the top cover around her and then, thinking that only half a job, she manoeuvred her slender form until she was beneath the it.

Hmm, lovely, she mused, taking a mental note to smooth the cover over before she left the room in a minute. In the meantime, what about Sloan Illingworth? Where on earth was he? Had his flight been delayed for some reason? Thinking of flying brought to mind Dermot's spending one Saturday—so he had said—picking up an aunt from an airport. Suddenly her head was stuffed with bitty pictures of a faceless Sloan Illingworth, of her father, of her mother, and of Dermot Selby, and as image after image fought for precedence, suddenly, to the background music of the raucous party below, Whitney fell asleep.

She stirred from her slumber, believing that she was in the middle of some nightmare. For indeed, nightmare just about covered what she awakened to. She was disturbed first by the sound of someone shrieking a shrill, 'Come on, you lot, you know I told you that the upstairs part of the house was taboo!' The next moment, before Whitney had any idea of where she was, someone had crashed into the bedroom, found the light switch, and flooded the room with light.

Having slept in the darkness to the accompaniment of loud music and a general din, the change from darkness to light, the change from the cacophony of noise she had slept through to the sudden silence—the sudden hushed silence—brought Whitney properly awake. And that was when the nightmare really began!

She was lying on her side when she surfaced to move one bare arm and shoulder from beneath the bedcover under which she found herself. Then she opened her eyes and, disbelieving, suddenly her eyes were wide. For, too stunned to move a muscle, she saw from the broad, naked shoulders that met her gaze that she was not in bed alone!

Before she could get muscular release from the spasm that gripped her, though, her bed companion made some exasperated sound and, thoroughly irritated, he sat up.

Whitney almost sat up too but, as a gasp from the region of the doorway hit her ears and her eyes caught sight of her own bare arm, she was all at once much too confused to know if she was as completely naked as her bed-fellow appeared to be, or not. She opted, for the moment, to freeze.

Though she did turn slightly so that she could see the door and see what that gasp was all about.

'You two-timing bastard!' assaulted her ears, and she saw that there was not just one person standing at the bedroom door, but a whole host of people surveying her and the man she was in bed with. 'My God! To think that, all these months, I've trusted you!' the shrill voice shrieked again and, as it isolated itself from the group by the door, Whitney recognised that the woman who was berating the man beside her was none other than her hostess, Gleda Caufield!

Whitney had never met Gleda's fiancé, Sloan Illingworth. But, as she turned her head to take in the mid-thirties, quite good-looking hunk of a man who was shaking his head as though to banish all sleep away— she had a very certain feeling that she just had!

CHAPTER TWO

WHITNEY did not have very long in which to study her fair-haired, grey-eyed host. For, her voice rising, Gleda Caufield had ceased berating her fiancé, and had switched to venting her spleen on her.

'As for you, you bitch,' she hissed, 'I hope you're satisfied that, through you, my engagement is over!'

'Y-you... I didn't... I'm...' Whitney was certain she hadn't done anything wrong, but, as though it was all part and parcel of the nightmare, she just seemed incapable of getting that message across. And then, somewhat to her relief, Sloan Illingworth was taking over.

Whitney guessed that he was mightily disturbed that his fiancée had just broken off their engagement because she saw him, heedless of who was about, snatch up the robe which had somehow mysteriously appeared at the end of the bed. Not quick enough to avert her eyes when she became aware of his intent, Whitney caught a glimpse of naked, muscular thigh as Sloan Illingworth, shrugging into the robe as he moved, uncurled his long length from the bed.

She was still staring, still stunned when he went over to his fiancée. Miraculously, everyone just seemed to melt away, and Whitney watched as, taking hold of Gleda's arm, Sloan Illingworth led her from the bedroom.

Whitney lay frozen for perhaps one minute more, then, overwhelmingly pleased to see that—as she had realised must be the case—she was still fully clad, she leapt from the bed.

Where to go, though? That was the immediate problem. If Sloan Illingworth was trying to get it through to Gleda that she had got it all wrong and that things weren't as they'd appeared when she had come into the bedroom, then matters weren't going to be helped if Gleda suddenly clapped eyes on *her*. Spotting an adjoining bathroom Whitney opted to cool her burning cheeks in there.

Ten minutes later, she had recovered a good deal of her deserted composure, but she was still hesitant about showing herself before Gleda and her fiancé had patched things up. The way things stood, she had done enough for tonight, albeit innocently. Never, though, had she thought to be a part of such a scene.

What Sloan Illingworth was doing going to bed when his fiancée had laid on a welcome-home party puzzled Whitney for a while. Then, recalling how Valerie had said something on the way down about his having been overseas busily establishing some new business, she supposed, what with flight delays and everything, that he must have come home exhausted.

Whitney was marginally grateful that she could remember seeing neither Valerie nor her brother Toby in the sea of interested faces at the bedroom doorway just now. Though without a doubt they would have heard what had happened.

She stayed in the bathroom for another ten minutes, time enough, she thought, in which for Sloan to have convinced Gleda that he was not the 'two-timer' she had called him.

Opening the bathroom door a crack, she listened. The silence, the peace, was deafening. Not quite believing that the house could be this peaceful after all the babble that had gone on, Whitney pulled the door open another inch or two. Then suddenly the peace was shattered.

'If you intend coming from that bathroom, then bloody well come!' snarled a disagreeable-sounding, all-male voice. 'I'd like to get *some* sleep tonight!'

Nervously, Whitney jerked the door the rest of the way open, but she had to swallow hard before she left the bathroom to confront the owner of that aggressive voice.

The owner, as she had suspected, was Sloan Illingworth. At least, she thought it was him. 'Y-you're Sl-Sloan Illingworth?' she questioned, finding that the broad, hair-roughened, otherwise naked chest of the man who sat up in bed was a degree or two off-putting.

'In the flesh,' he answered without humour. His gaze took her in from the top of her dark head to the tips of her shoeless toes. 'You managed to find your clothes, I see.'

It took Whitney a second or two to get on to his wave-length. 'I never lost them,' she told him quickly as it registered that, for all she had not been aware of him looking at her, this man had not only done so, but had also registered that she had seemed as naked as he. 'Actually,' she added primly, 'but for the fact that some lout broke the strap of my dress earlier this evening, I've not parted with any of my clothes the whole time I've been here. Except for my shoes,' she added hurriedly.

'Are you bragging or complaining?' he mocked.

Whitney decided right then that she did not like Mr Sloan Illingworth, and, intent upon ignoring him, she stooped down looking for her shoes. She found them just under the bed, and she lost no time in putting them on. She was a little taller than average, but even so, even while Sloan Illingworth was sitting while she stood, Whitney felt better for having added a couple of inches to her height.

Belatedly though, even while not liking him, and even though she knew that he was waiting for her to leave so that he could get some sleep, she realised that she owed him an apology.

'I'm—sorry,' she said as levelly as she could as she took a step towards the door. 'I know I shouldn't have come in here and made free with your bed, but . . .'

'You were alone?' he queried, making her blood pressure soar.

'Of course I was alone!' she snapped.

'You weren't enjoying the party?' he asked, masterly with the quickness of his conclusions, she observed.

'It—isn't—er—the sort of party I'm used to,' she found herself explaining in the politest terms, since it was his fiancée who had thrown the event.

'Which was why you decided to go to bed?'

'Not intentionally!' she denied, and before she could think about it, 'I didn't hear you come to bed,' she added.

'I tried not to disturb you,' he replied, and had she not known better she would have sworn there was a grin at the back of the remark just dying to get through.

'You knew I was there!' she exclaimed, taking his remark at face-value.

'Actually,' he drawled, 'no.'

'Oh,' she said dully, and realised that he must think that she was as thick as two short planks that she hadn't cottoned on to his sense of humour. 'Well, anyway,' she said, taking another step towards the door, 'I'm sorry about that, and I'm—er—sorry that Gleda was upset— which is only natural,' she inserted quickly, 'but now

that everything's all right again and you're engaged once
more, I'll...'

'Now where,' Sloan Illingworth interrupted, 'did you
get the impression that I'm once more engaged to be
married?'

'You're—not?' Whitney gasped, halting abruptly, and
taking a step back into the room.

He shook his head, 'Not,' he stated.

'Oh, dear,' Whitney fretted, as she realised that Gleda
had been too upset to listen to his explanation. 'I'm
sorry,' she said again, and, accepting that she could say
she was sorry until she was blue in the face, but that
that still would not get his engagement mended, she told
him firmly, 'I'll go and see Gleda. I'll make her understand that you were entirely blameless and that you didn't
even know that I was in that bed when you...' She came
to a stop when she realised that she should be explaining
all this to the woman he loved. 'I'll go now,' she said
determinedly, and made to turn towards the door.

'Where, might one ask,' his voice arrested her, 'are
you going?'

'Why, downstairs, of course,' Whitney told him. 'I'll
ask Gleda if I can have a few words with her and...'

'If you're hoping to find my ex-fiancée downstairs,
I'm afraid you're in for a disappointment,' he cut her
off. 'She's gone.'

'Gone!' Whitney repeated blankly. 'But...'

'As the rest of her friends have gone.'

'The rest of her...' Whitney was gasping as what he
was saying began to sink in.

'The party, as they say in the song,' he told her ur-
banely, 'is over.'

'Over!'

'You really will have to keep off the bird seed,' Sloan Illingworth murmured sarcastically.

Whitney ignored his hardly veiled suggestion that by repeating everything he said she was sounding just like a parrot, and she summoned some aggression of her own. He wasn't as clever as he thought he was. 'Over or not,' she snapped, 'not everyone can have left, because the people I came with will have stayed behind to give me a lift back to London.'

Sloan Illingworth was so sure of himself that he did not even ask who she had come with. 'Take my word for it,' he told her, his tone short in response to her uppity manner, 'there's no one left.'

'How do you know there's no one left?' she questioned him hostilely.

'Because I watched the last car leave!' he rapped.

That he had lost any small sign of being affable and was now revealing a hint of anger was no more than she should expect, Whitney realised. After all, she had been instrumental in causing his fiancée to break off their engagement. But, for the moment, Whitney had a more pressing problem than helping him and his fiancée get back together again.

'But,' she cried, 'if Toby and his sister have gone— I've no way of getting home!'

The look which Sloan Illingworth threw her told her that he couldn't have cared less about Toby, or about Toby's sister, or about her. It was clear that he thought that her predicament was nothing to do with him. But it seemed that his need to close his eyes had got to him.

'For God's sake!' he barked, and obviously seeing nothing for it but to find a solution, he snarled, 'Go and clear up downstairs or something! I'll see about getting you home when I've caught up on some sleep.'

A little taken aback, Whitney realised that she was going nowhere until this uncivil brute had made friends with Morpheus. Still, she had hardly thought she would be staying to clear up when she had accepted the invitation to the party.

'You want me to clear up after...'

'I don't see why the hell my housekeeper should do it!' he told her shortly. Dawn was creeping through the night sky when he commanded, 'Put the light out on your way,' and, turning his back on her, concluded their conversation by lying down and, she presumed, closing his eyes.

Hoping that he would awake in a better mood, Whitney snicked the light switch off as she left the bedroom. Miserable creature, she muttered under her breath, and observed how every one of the hurdles that should have prevented all but the most steady-footed from negotiating the stairs had been removed. More than likely, Sloan Illingworth had removed the hurdles when he had come home, Whitney thought. She was warned of the state in which she would find the other rooms when she saw how liberally strewn with debris the hall was. She had not seriously contemplated doing any of the clearing up but, as she walked through the other rooms the guests had used, she could not help but agree with the brute of a man upstairs. No housekeeper should have to come on duty to a house looking like this!

Realising that she would wear a trench to the kitchen if she attempted to take the used dishes there by tray, Whitney found a trolley and was soon hard at work.

Her mood during the next hour swung many ways. She countered her belief that Sloan Illingworth was a miserable creature with the feeling that, with his welcome

home after three months away being a broken engagement, he had every right to be upset.

Having cleared the hall of all the clutter, she decided
to wash up the dishes and glasses she found there before
she went on to the next disaster area. There was a dishwasher plumbed in beside the sink, but it was a make
she was not familiar with, and Whitney decided against
using it in case she turned a wrong knob and wrecked
the machine.

She was up to her elbows in soapsuds when she began
to feel belligerent again. Who else, in their right mind,
would skivvy away at the kitchen sink at five o'clock on
a Sunday morning? On that instant, Whitney took her
hands out of the suds and, rebelling, she dried them.

Five minutes later, her hands were in the water again.
It was one thing to think, blow Sloan Illingworth, let
him do his own washing up; but quite another to keep
down a conscience which insisted, ah, but he won't have
to do it, will he? Whitney could not remember seeing
any sign of his housekeeper, but it was a fair bet that
she would be the one lumbered with the clearing up if
she didn't do it. And, as that short-tempered creature
upstairs had stated, why the hell should she?

Whitney still didn't see why *she* should be the person
to be lumbered with the chores, but beneath all her
strongly antagonistic feeling there lay a much stronger
feeling of guilt. For, through her, however innocent she
was, Sloan Illingworth had lost the woman he loved.
And Whitney knew how it felt to lose the person you
loved.

That the two cases were in no way similar made no
difference to that deep-down feeling of guilt, she discovered. She had been the one to throw Dermot over,

not the other way around as in Sloan's case, but that in no way lessened the hurt.

Whitney finished her first load of washing-up and left the kitchen to begin work in the drawing-room. She had just managed to get rid of the last ring-mark on a highly polished table when she took a minute out to look round at the rest of the beautiful furniture in the room. Feeling slightly amazed that the housekeeper had agreed that that unmannered partying horde be let loose among such surroundings, she suddenly realised that she probably hadn't had much choice.

She hadn't particularly taken to Gleda Caufield herself, but she had no need to see her again. As things had stood, though, since Gleda Caufield was due ultimately to be the mistress of Heathlands, when the housekeeper would permanently take her instructions from her, Whitney saw that the housekeeper had little option but to agree.

Feeling guilty again for her part in depriving Heathlands of its expected mistress, Whitney started on more washing-up. She fervently hoped that, once Gleda Caufield had cooled down, Sloan would be able to get her to see reason.

At seven-fifteen, Whitney thought she deserved a cup of tea, and she set the kettle to boil. She was in the middle of her first rest when a woman of about fifty came briskly into the kitchen and, seeing her taking her ease, stopped dead.

'Good morning,' Whitney smiled. 'I hope you don't mind me making free with your teapot. I'm Whitney Lawford, by the way.'

'How do you do,' the woman replied and, after introducing herself, 'I'm Mrs Orton, Mr Illingworth's housekeeper,' she added, a shade warily, Whitney thought, 'Are—er—there other—er—guests still here?'

'No, only me,' Whitney soon put her out of her anxiety, and, drawing a thick veil over the happenings in that upstairs bedroom, added, 'I sort of—got left behind—when everyone else went home.'

'I—see,' Mrs Orton murmured, although she didn't really look as though she did.

'Mr Illingworth has said he'll see about getting me home, once he's caught up on some of his rest,' Whitney found she was explaining.

'He's a kind man,' Mrs Orton offered.

Perhaps he treats his housekeeper kindly, Whitney mused, but so far she had seen more of his bad-tempered side than his kind side. 'I thought I'd have a cup of tea, and then I'd do some clearing up,' she decided to change the subject.

'Oh, I can't let you do that,' Mrs Orton protested, all too clearly unaware that the good fairies had been slaving away for the past three hours. 'Besides, I've just taken a look around, and the house is nowhere near as—er—untidy as I imagined it would be.' With that, and giving her the impression that she would be a shade happier to have her kitchen all to herself, the housekeeper set about finding the right homes for the dishes which Whitney had washed.

'I'll take my tea into the drawing-room,' Whitney told her, not wanting to get under Mrs Orton's feet if she was the sort who went about her duties with bustling speed.

'Shall I make you some breakfast?' the housekeeper relented.

'Oh no, thanks, Mrs Orton,' Whitney replied. 'I couldn't eat a thing,'

Nor could she. What she wanted more than food,
Whitney realised as she took a seat on the comfortable-
looking couch in the drawing-room and finished her tea,
was eight hours of solid sleep.

Suddenly aware of a feeling of tiredness, Whitney
placed her cup and saucer down on a nearby table and
kicked off her shoes. Stretching out on the couch, she
thought that Mrs Orton had enough to keep her busy
elsewhere, and, since it could well be mid-afternoon
before Sloan Illingworth surfaced, she could see no good
reason why she shouldn't catch up on some of her sleep
too.

This time when she came round from sleep, it was not
to find herself looking at the broad, naked shoulders of
Sloan Illingworth. This time, she opened her eyes to look
straight up into his watching grey eyes and, suddenly,
as she saw him standing tall, with his broad shoulders
covered in a checked shirt, Whitney's heart set up the
most unexpected thudding.

'What time is it?' she asked him as she sat up and
slipped her feet into her shoes and wondered why seeing
him dressed should have affected her so much that she
didn't have the brain power to check her own watch.

'Getting on for ten,' he replied, affably enough, she
thought, given the way she had ruined his future.

'Has Gleda—your fiancée—your ex-fiancée,' she
qualified, 'rung?'

'Why the deuce should she?' he derided, making her
realise that perhaps she wasn't so instantly wide awake
as she had thought.

'I'm sorry,' she apologised, and experienced a rush of
irritation with him, and with herself, that he seemed
without effort to have her in a constant state of apologising to him. To counteract any thought he might have

that she went through life grovelling, she snapped bluntly, 'Can we go now?'

'Where the hell to?' he rapped back, equally bluntly.

'You said you'd give me a lift to...'

'I want my breakfast!' he snarled, and seemed about to stride off when he checked. 'I suppose I'd better feed you, too. Come on,' he said shortly.

Whitney was about to tell him what he could do with his food, but as he reached down and hauled her unceremoniously to her feet she was overtaken by a sudden feeling of breathlessness. All at once she was very much aware of him and the way he towered over her. Quickly, she took a smart step away.

By the time she had recovered her equilibrium, he was escorting her along the hall and, since she just then discovered that she was starving, the moment was lost when she would have told him that he could eat by himself.

The room he took her to was one she had not been in before, and she guessed that it must be one of the rooms which Mrs Orton had thought to lock before the invasion of last night.

Sloan Illingworth had an innate courtesy, Whitney was to find. For, even while annoyed with her, as he undoubtedly was, he had pulled out a chair for her at the breakfast table and was waiting for her to be seated before he went round to his own chair.

'Thank you,' she mumbled, and had some minutes in which to compose herself while Mrs Orton brought in two plates of bacon and egg.

The housekeeper had gone out again, and Whitney's host was tucking into the delicious-smelling repast, as she was, when she thought that, since she had annoyed him the last time she'd started to ask for a lift to London, perhaps she had better use a bit of tact the next time.

Realising that probably the only reason he had turned grumpy was that he had other things planned for that day than seeing to it that she got back to her home, Whitney found that to be beholden to him had made her, conversely, short on tact.

'Shall I?' she offered pleasantly, touching her hand to the coffee-pot handle.

His terse nod made it harder than ever for her to find tact to ask him anything. She just hated asking for favours. Yet, since she didn't want to spend much more time cooling her heels at Heathlands—nor could he want her there anyway, she was sure of that—Whitney daintily poured them both a cup of coffee.

She handed him his with a faint trace of a smile. 'Mr Illingworth,' she began, keeping her voice as pleasant as before. She halted when she found that grey eyes were suddenly pinning hers. As she stared at him, it struck her that if she did not know better, she would have sworn there was the very devil dancing in those grey eyes!

'Mr Illingworth?' he queried. Her expression must have told him that she didn't consider she knew him well enough to call him by his first name. But he left her stunned and gaping when, copying her own pleasantness of tone, he murmured, 'After sleeping with me, I'm still Mr Illingworth to you?'

'You—you... I...' Whitney spluttered, and she was never more glad that there was no one around to hear this conversation.

'Come to think of it,' Sloan Illingworth went on when Whitney proved too choked to get more words out, 'I've been more than remiss in the name department myself. Tell me,' he went on, 'since I was such a cad as not to ask beforehand, what *is* the name of the woman I so recently had the pleasure of sleeping with?'

Discounting the idea that there was any devil dancing in his eyes, Whitney realised that the only reason for him bringing up the subject of them being in the same bed together was that Gleda must be to the forefront of his mind. Burned on his brain must be the picture of him waking up to find his fiancée standing in the bedroom doorway, shocked and dreadfully upset that, after organising a surprise party for him, the surprise had been to find him in bed with one of the guests.

'My name is Whitney Lawford,' she told him flatly, and, when she had been determined not to apologise again, 'I'm sorry, I really am,' she just had to tell him.

'You're sorry you found the party so unutterably boring that, since you had no transport to leave, you decided to hide yourself away where you thought no one would find you?'

She had been apologising for the shock she had caused his ex-fiancée. But his outline of the way her thoughts had gone, if not very polite to her hostess, was pretty near accurate.

'I hadn't meant to go to sleep,' she muttered. 'And I certainly didn't know it was your bedroom when I...'

'It seems to me that you didn't give a damn whose bedroom it was, or what—upsetting—consequences might follow your actions,' Sloan retorted toughly.

The memory of her own upset, her own pain from her break with Dermot, was enough to keep Whitney's eyes glued to her plate. She had no defence, she knew that she hadn't. But she did not want to see the pain she had known mirrored in the grey eyes of the man opposite her because, through no fault of his own, his love had broken with him.

'Can't...' she began huskily, but the words to ask him if he didn't think he could get back together again with

Gleda just refused to leave her throat. Whitney coughed to clear a constriction, and then found herself saying something very different from what she had intended. Pride, she could only surmise, was responsible for the non-grovelling person who raised her head from her plate and, tilting her chin a defiant fraction, told him evenly, 'Since my actions have resulted in such disastrous happenings for you, I don't suppose I can complain that you have obviously had second thoughts about helping me get back to London.' Quietly, and with dignity, Whitney placed her napkin on her side-plate. 'So, since I have to be at my secretarial job in the morning, I'll thank you for—for . . . your hospitality, and I'll start . . .'

'Did I say I'd had second thoughts?' he sliced in bluntly.

'No, but . . .'

'Then kindly don't jump to conclusions about what I think or how I think or anything else about me,' he told her cuttingly. 'I've told you I'll see about getting you home, and that's my intention.'

Whitney did not like the feeling that she had just been well and truly slapped down for her impudence. 'Very well,' she told him stiffly. 'But since, when I put this dress on yesterday evening, I didn't think that I'd be spending the whole of today in it too, can you give me some idea of how long it will be before I can get home to my flat, to a bath and a change of clothes?'

His answer was to toss his serviette down on the table too. Not looking the least bit friendly, he told her disagreeably, 'Give me ten minutes to get some paperwork together, and we'll be off.'

'You're going to your office!' she exclaimed.

Without another word Sloan Illingworth got up from the table and strode from the room, and Whitney fell back into her sour mood. Leaving the breakfast-room, she wandered out into the hall.

True to his word, ten minutes later, Sloan came and found her. The briefcase he carried confirmed, as she had thought, that he would be calling in at his office once he had dropped her off. Unspeaking, they went from the house, and silently he opened the passenger door of his dark, sleek and speedy-looking car.

In no time Heathlands was miles behind them. Dearly did Whitney wish she could put the happenings at Heathlands as quickly to the back of her. Nothing but a grim silence was coming from the man behind the wheel, and she supposed that she could hardly blame him that he'd rather be giving a lift to a wart-ridden crone, just then, than her.

As they neared London she told him where she lived, and he took that information in without acknowledgement. Whitney looked out of the side-window, and tried hard to hate him. But guilt was cutting deeper, and hate him she could not.

She guessed that, for all he was not outwardly showing it, he was being torn apart inside about Gleda. And, suddenly, her own pain over Dermot was being magnified and was causing her heart to go out to Sloan.

Whitney was still feeling for him when, after she had given him a few further directions, he pulled his car up outside of her flat. And, somehow, although she thought she read in his expression that he would be glad if she'd get out of the car so that he could get on, she just had to delay him.

'Sloan,' she said huskily, the 'Mr Illingworth' which she had previously called him lost somewhere under her urgent need to help him patch up his broken engagement. Coolly, he turned his head to survey her earnest expression. 'Sloan,' she repeated quickly, and there was a nervous catch in her voice when, emotion taking her along, she almost begged, 'if there's anything I can do, *anything* at all . . .'

Her voice faded to nothing as, with one eyebrow slanting aloft, Sloan Illingworth told her icily, 'Some might say, Miss Lawford, that you've done more than enough already!'

CHAPTER THREE

Toby Keston was waiting for Whitney when she arrived at her office the following morning, and he was abject in his apologies when he begged her forgiveness for abandoning her at the party.

'I didn't mean to, I swear I didn't,' he said earnestly. 'I was taking care how much I was drinking, too. Only,' he ended miserably, 'some idiot got the bright idea of lacing my drinks, and—well, I couldn't remember very much about the party when I woke up in my flat yesterday afternoon.'

'You—er—must have been in a state,' Whitney murmured carefully as she wondered if any of what he remembered included the fact that Sloan Illingworth was no longer engaged to be married, and that she was the cause!

'I was in a worse state when I rang my sister to ask how I'd got home, and she told me that she'd driven *me* home, but not *you*! I was in a proper stew when she said how she'd got some chap to pour me into her car and to go with her to help her at the other end, but that she'd left you to get a lift with someone else. You did get a lift without any problem, didn't you?' he asked anxiously.

'Oh, yes,' Whitney replied, still wondering how much he knew.

'Oh, good,' he said on a relieved breath, and added, 'I wanted to come round to your place yesterday to see if you were home safely but, well, to tell the truth, I had a splitting head, and I wasn't at all sure what sort of reception you'd give me.' He paused, and then asked tentatively, 'The chap who gave you a lift—he was all right, was he? I mean,' he added, 'he didn't try...'

'He was fine,' Whitney relieved his mind, while at the same time she held back from informing him that the man who had given her a lift home was the man who had been his host for the evening. 'Er—what time did you leave, by the way?' she questioned Toby, a touch tentative herself.

'I've no idea,' he replied. 'Though it must have been before Gleda Caufield's fiancé arrived, because Valerie gave me an earful yesterday about how, through me, she'd missed the best part of the party.'

'Oh,' said Whitney weakly, and found that she just did not have the nerve to ask him what his sister had meant by that remark. Had she meant the best part had been when the host of the surprise party had arrived, or had she meant—word having already reached her ears— that the best part had been when quite a few of the crowd had surprised their host in bed with one of the guests?

Fortunately, Whitney's boss just then arrived. 'Good morning, Mr Parsons,' Toby greeted him in the same good-natured way in which he spoke to everyone, and, as he recalled that Mr Parsons had a reputation for not caring for time-wasters, 'I'll see you later, Whitney,' he smiled, and went on his way.

Whitney quite liked her work at Alford Plastics, but it was not too demanding work, so that throughout that day she had plenty of time in which to let her mind run free. Over and over again she thought of everything that had taken place since she had gone to that party with Toby on Saturday. Dearly did she want to know if Sloan Illingworth had been able to patch things up with his fiancée, but, short of getting in touch with him to ask, she had no way of knowing.

She was still fretting over the fact that through her innocent act two people who were in love had been caused pain, when she went home that night. She was wishing that she could know if the engagement had been mended when, at about eleven when she was thinking of going to bed, her upstairs neighbour came and knocked her well-known knock on her door.

Erica Fane was a warm-hearted woman of thirty who, while holding down a demanding job, was studying for a degree with the Open University. While efficient in her job, and in her studies, however, Erica tended to be forgetful in other smaller matters.

Whitney opened the door to her, well used by then to the peculiar hours which Erica's studies meant she kept. 'What can I . . . ?' Whitney began, but she stopped when Erica waved a tin of sardines in the air.

'I'm not on the cadge tonight, I'm returning,' she beamed.

'Come in, if you've time,' Whitney invited.

'Don't mind if I do,' Erica replied, and they adjourned to the kitchen where Whitney made two mugs of cocoa, and where Erica said, 'I'm dying to pry—where were you on Saturday when, sardines in hand, I came knocking at your door?'

'Come and sit down, and I'll tell you,' Whitney answered.

'Crumbs!' Erica exclaimed when Whitney had given her an outline of how she had come to be found in bed with Sloan Illingworth when Gleda Caufield had come into the room. 'You're just not the type!'

'I'll take that as flattery,' Whitney said drily. 'But— what can I do?'

'As I see it, nothing, kiddo,' Erica told her. 'You say you offered to do anything you can, but, well, quite honestly, if I'd caught my feller—I should be so lucky—in bed with some female, then the last person I'd want to see would be said female. Leave it,' she advised. 'Love, as you know, poppet,' she inserted gently, being the only person in whom Whitney had confided over Dermot, 'is a pretty powerful emotion. They'll get back together again, I'm sure, if they haven't already.'

Whitney carried Erica's advice with her when she went into work the next day. She was still trying to convince herself that everything was back to normal on the Sloan and Gleda front though when, on her way to the coffee machine around mid-morning, Toby Keston fell into step with her.

'I was hoping to see you,' he smiled, and while Whitney's guilty conscience gave a start that word must have reached him of her being found in bed with Sloan Illingworth, he went on to say, 'I'd like you to go out with me again, but I don't suppose you would—would you?'

Whitney faced the fact that she had a decided aversion to such a sordid phrase as her 'being found in bed' with anyone, and relief that Toby still knew nothing of what was now becoming an irritant to her was responsible, she realised, for her reply.

'Provided you're not thinking of taking me to any more parties...' she began when, his face lighting up like a beacon in his pleasure, Toby snapped up what he saw as her acceptance of a date.

Whitney dated Toby several times over the next two weeks. When, at the end of their third date, though, he made an attempt to kiss her, she quickly averted her head and his kiss landed on her cheek.

'No?' he asked.

'No, Toby,' she told him firmly. 'I told you...'

'I know, you're "off" men,' he repeated what she had told him and, like the love he was, he had confessed, 'I tried it on, despite what you told me. Will you forgive me and come out with me again if I promise to behave myself?'

Whitney knew then that she liked Toby very much. He wasn't asking why she was 'off' men, he just accepted that she was. 'Who could resist you?' she smiled.

'My mother thinks I'm cute,' he replied, and Whitney laughed, and when by the end of their next date Toby had not so much as attempted to hold her hand, she knew that, in a sisterly kind of way, she had grown quite fond of Toby.

She was at work on a Friday morning, almost three weeks to the day since Toby had taken her to that party, when she put down a piece of work she had been going over and stared into space. She was beginning to think that that party was going to haunt her for the rest of her life, because somehow never a day seemed to pass without Sloan Illingworth popping into her head at some time. Ejecting him, along with her guilty conscience, from her thoughts, she picked up her work again. For goodness' sake, he'd had time to explain everything to Gleda Caufield a dozen times over by now! By now, she decided, everything *must* have settled down between the pair of them. She was not going to give them another thought.

An hour later, Sloan Illingworth was far from Whitney's mind. When the phone on her desk rang she had her thoughts more on supply dates than on who was at the other end of the phone.

Then, suddenly, her work had gone completely from her mind, and she was shaken to the core as the deep tones of an all-male voice enquired, 'How are you, Whitney?' She had never before heard Sloan Illingworth's voice over the phone, but she nevertheless knew straight away who it was.

'I'm—fine,' she replied as evenly as her shaken senses would allow.

'Good,' he said and, having got that out of the way, 'Sloan Illingworth,' he announced himself, and without further preamble told her, 'I should like to see you.'

'Oh!' she exclaimed, having thought that she had got herself together again, only to be shaken once more by what he had just said. 'You mean...' Her voice faded. In a flash she was realising that, since he did not want to talk to her over the phone, what he wanted to see her about must be exceedingly personal. With a start she realised too that her belief that his broken engagement had been patched up must be very wide of the mark! And, suddenly remembering her offer of doing anything to help, Whitney all at once knew that she could not withdraw that offer, which Sloan was calling in. 'Er—yes,' she told him, 'all right. I...' She had been about to tell him that she was free from one till two and that she could meet him anywhere he said in her lunch hour, but she didn't get the chance. For, waiting no longer than to hear her agree that she would see him, Sloan Illingworth, clearly a very busy man, wasted no more of his time, but cut straight across anything she was adding.

'I'll see you tonight, at eight. We'll eat somewhere,' he said. A moment later, Whitney was staring, in some disbelief, at the dead telephone in her hand.

'My giddy aunt!' she exclaimed aloud, and replaced the receiver, feeling her hackles start to rise at the bossy treatment she had just received.

Mutiny welled up in her as she recalled that she had a date with Toby that night, but that the lordly Sloan Illingworth hadn't even thought to ask if it was convenient when he'd stated, 'I'll see you tonight, at eight'!

Wishing that she had thought to take his phone number so that she could have rung him back and told him that tonight was not convenient, Whitney quietly simmered against him for the next few minutes.

Presumptuous blighter! she fumed. So what if she had put him in the wrong with his fiancée? She already had a date for that evening! For all Sloan Illingworth knew, he could well have ruined a budding romance on *her* horizon!

Thoughts of a romance in any way connected with her caused Whitney to think of Dermot. And, as sadness entered her heart, so anger left her. Dermot had been her one and only foray into anything remotely approaching a serious romance—she was definitely not ready for another.

Whitney picked up the phone to ring Toby's extension, having accepted that, after what she'd done to Sloan's romance, he could hardly be blamed for not caring a damn whether he scuppered any budding romance she had going.

'Toby—Whitney here,' she told him when he came to the phone.

'Hello!' he exclaimed, and she could hear the pleasure in his voice.

'About tonight,' she began, and then she hesitated. She had got to know Toby sufficiently well by then, and knew that he was open enough to have mentioned it had he been aware of Sloan Illingworth's broken engagement, and her part in it. Somehow, she didn't feel like giving Toby the real reason why she could not see him that evening. 'I'm sorry, Toby,' she resumed, 'something's come up and I can't make our date tonight.'

'You're not in trouble, are you, Whitney?' he immediately asked, causing her to like him all the more that his first thought was always for others. 'If something's wrong, you know you can rely on me to...'

'There's nothing wrong,' she quickly told him, and when an embarrassed pause followed when she didn't explain why she was cancelling their date, she found that she was saying, 'I'm sorry I can't make tonight, but if you're free tomorrow evening, perhaps you'd like to come and have dinner with me at my place.'

'Would I!' Toby jumped at her invitation, adding, in some relief, 'I thought for a minute there that you were saying that you didn't want to see me ever again, not just tonight.'

'You're getting touchy in your old age,' Whitney teased him, and she had almost returned the phone to its cradle when, on an afterthought, she said, 'Oh, by the way, where can I get in contact with Sloan Illingworth, do you know?'

'Since you know where he lives, it has to be business,' Toby said cheerfully, and in happy ignorance, he told her, 'You've heard of Illingworth International; try there. He runs it.'

Whitney put the phone down in something of a state of shock. Sloan Illingworth was head of Illingworth International, that vast multinational company! And she—she had a date with him that night!

It took Whitney until some time after her lunch hour to get over the shock of learning who Sloan Illingworth was. She had known he was an industrialist, she recalled, but never had she connected him with the Illingworth who presided over the Illingworth International board.

Whitney went home that night realising that, if some wisp of memory hadn't strayed to remind her, while she was talking to Toby, that she hadn't known where to contact Sloan, she would never have asked Toby the question she had. As it was, she knew not only that he ran Illingworth International but also, since the name Illingworth could not be coincidental, that he owned it.

Pattering about her flat prior to taking a bath, she was still thinking of how she had so unknowingly trotted out her question to find out where Sloan worked, when, like a bolt from the blue, something suddenly hit her. She knew how she had found out where Sloan worked— but how had he found out where *she* worked?

Whitney was still racking her brains when, half an hour later, she lay soaking in her bath. She had a good memory of several of the things that had passed between them. And she could clearly remember telling him she did secretarial work. But she was positive she had not told him where!

She got out of her bath telling herself that whether she had told Sloan where she worked or whether she hadn't was not all that important anyway. He knew her address, so, if all else had failed, all he'd had to do was either drop her a note asking her to phone him, or call round in person to see her. The fact that he hadn't forgotten where she lived was endorsed by the fact that, without asking for a reminder, he was calling at her address that evening.

Knowing for certain that Sloan would not have telephoned her if his engagement to Gleda was still on,

Whitney was donning the dress she would wear when, as she recalled to mind his tall, lithe build and his good-looking face, she was suddenly visited by the most peculiar sensation.

How ridiculous, she thought, and, scorning the idea that the sensation had been anything to do with excitement at the thought of having him for her escort, she smoothed the folds of the pale amber silk around her hips, and stepped into her shoes.

At eight o'clock precisely, she was seated in an easy chair, ready and waiting. She was perfectly cool, calm and collected. At one minute past eight, the outside bell to her flat rang, and suddenly she felt decidedly jumpy.

Picking up her bag, Whitney went from her flat, and locked the door behind her. Then she took a deep breath and negotiated the stairs to the ground floor. She had herself under control as she reached the outer door, or thought she had. But, just the same, she discovered that she needed to take another deep breath before she pulled the door back.

'A punctual woman!' Sloan exclaimed before she could speak, observing from the way she toted her bag that he was not going to be asked in to wait. 'A beautiful and punctual woman,' he rephrased his observation.

Funnily enough, the words on his lips did not seem to her ears to be insincere flattery, and, as Sloan took possession of her elbow and escorted her to the luxurious car standing at the kerb, Whitney experienced that most peculiar sensation again.

Oh, all right, then, she conceded when with her seated next to him Sloan drove off; maybe it was excitement that gripped her. But what was wrong with that? 'Where are we going?' she asked him as she accepted that the last time she had felt anywhere near like she was feeling now was when she had gone out with Dermot.

Sloan kept his eyes on the road ahead as he told her the name of a smart and wildly expensive restaurant. 'Is that all right with you?' he enquired.

'Fine—fine,' Whitney replied, having received the distinct impression that she had only to say the word and he would have taken her elsewhere to dine. It was then that she realised that Sloan Illingworth was the most suave and sophisticated man she had ever met. For the fact that he had conveyed that impression, without having to state outright that he would take her to an alternative restaurant if she preferred, seemed to say it all.

Perhaps, she mused, when shortly afterwards she was sitting across the table from him in the restaurant, it was all part and parcel of his sophistication that she in no way felt uncomfortable or awkward at being in his illustrious company, or in such smart surroundings. She was not so dim, though, that she did not understand that he was more bent on putting her at her ease than really wanting to know the answers to the questions he asked her over their starter course. He was trying to bring her out by asking more about her.

Realising, as she did, that he was only being polite as a lead-up to what he wanted to ask with regard to enlisting her aid over his ex-fiancée, Whitney saw no harm in getting things on an affable footing.

'What can I tell you?' she played along with him. 'I work at Alford Plastics as secretary to a Mr Parsons, and I...' Suddenly she broke off. 'How did you know I worked at Alford Plastics, by the way? I'm sure I never said where I worked, and...'

'You didn't,' Sloan confirmed. 'What you did do, though, was to mention a Toby and his sister.'

'You know Toby Keston?' Even as the question left her, Whitney was wondering why Toby had not told her if Sloan had rung him to ask if he knew where she worked. Especially when, after breaking her date with Toby for that night, she had more or less asked him exactly that same question in reverse—did he know where Sloan Illingworth worked? But it was not Toby who had told Sloan where she might be found from nine to five on a weekday, she was to discover.

'I know young Keston about as well as I knew his chalk-from-cheese sister,' Sloan informed her, and went on to leave Whitney fairly open-mouthed when he enlightened her, 'I couldn't see you being a friend of Valerie Keston, which left you, in my opinion, as being a friend of her brother. Now where, I asked, would a man like him meet a woman like you?'

'You decided he'd met me at his place of work?' Whitney suggested faintly. 'You rang him and...'

'I decided that you both must work for the same firm,' Sloan agreed. 'The trick was to remember where he worked.'

'You didn't ring him to ask...'

'I rang Alford Plastics and asked to speak with Miss Whitney Lawford.'

'You know,' Whitney said, when a few moments of digesting what he had said had sunk in, 'I'm not at all surprised that you're the head of a large international concern.'

'I think that's a compliment, but I'm not sure,' Sloan said, and for the first time Whitney witnessed that he had the most fabulous grin.

Her eyes went down to her empty plate, and just then the waiter came to their table. The second course had been served when Whitney looked at Sloan again. 'Er——'she said, but the question she wanted to ask would not stay down, and she just had to enquire, 'Why, by the way, couldn't you see me as being a friend of Valerie Keston?'

For a moment, Whitney thought that he was not going to answer, but suddenly a warm look had crept into the steady grey eyes that studied her face. 'You're poles apart,' he replied seriously.

It was the warm look in his eyes that did it, Whitney realised. For, encouraged by that look, she could not resist returning, 'I think that's a compliment, but I'm not sure.' Oddly, her heart gave a happy skip when, revealing that she had amused him, Sloan did not merely grin, but laughed. She discovered that she liked the sound.

'You're right, of course,' he told her when his amusement had faded. And while Whitney was realising that she was glad that he had not lumped her in the same hard and brittle class as Valerie Keston, he was saying, 'I can't see many, if any of the females at that party three weeks ago risking their nail polish to clear up the way you did.'

She was a little shaken on two fronts at once. But Whitney firstly decided that he must mean any of the females except his ex-fiancée, Gleda. And then, having not forgotten that Mrs Orton had no idea of the tidying up she had done, she questioned him about the second. 'Apart from my receiving explicit orders that you didn't see—er—why the hell—your housekeeper should clear up, how do you know that I did any of it?'

'Apart from my being certain that you wouldn't hesitate to tell me what to do with my "explicit orders" if you felt like it,' Sloan batted back at her, 'I knew you'd been hard at it from the moment Mrs Orton reported how Miss Caufield's guests had put everything "to rights" before they'd departed.' It was the first time during the evening that he had mentioned his ex-fiancée, but the moment when Whitney would have brought up the subject of why she was dining with him at all was lost, when he continued, 'My memory of it after everyone had gone was that it looked more as though a tornado had whipped through the downstairs, rather than it being put "to rights".'

'Oh,' she mumbled as she comprehended his deductions. 'Well,' she said, looking for an excuse to cover her actions, 'I just couldn't leave it as it was for your unsuspecting housekeeper to find.'

'See what I mean?' Sloan murmured, and Whitney was thinking that he had just re-endorsed his compliment, saying that she was poles apart from Valerie Keston who wouldn't have cared a button what state the place was in for the housekeeper to find, when Sloan continued, 'So you work at Alford Plastics. What happened before that?'

Whitney had to think fast to catch up with him, and to see that he had gone back to the beginning—almost as if he really was interested to know more about her. But, although she was certain that he could not possibly be that interested, she was experiencing the pain of remembering what had happened before she went to work at Alford Plastics.

'Before Alford's, I worked at Hobson's Garden Implements,' she said brightly—perhaps a shade too brightly. 'And before that, I lived in Cambridge with my parents. Only...' her voice faltered '...only when my mother died, and my father remarried, I thought it was about time I stood on my own two feet. So I came to London.'

'You didn't get on with your stepmother?' Sloan questioned.

But suddenly, Whitney pulled herself together. She did not know what it was about Sloan Illingworth; but, though she hardly knew the man, and though she had always thought of herself as rather a private person, here she was giving him a potted version of her life history!

'I got on with her quite well, actually,' she told him coolly, but she found that she just had to add, her cool tone gone, 'But home—just wasn't the same any more after my mother died.'

Realising that Sloan had done it again and once more had her revealing that which only her close confidante, Erica, knew, Whitney was just about to place the personal ball firmly in his court by asking how she could help him with regard to his ex-fiancée when he again shook her with his powers of perception.

'Who was he?' he asked.

'Who?' she queried, completely mystified. Her breath was completely taken away at his reply.

'The man at Hobson's Garden Implements who hurt you,' he answered.

'How do you kn...' she started to fire when she had her breath back, but since she had as good as admitted that she had been hurt by some man at her old place of employment, Whitney tilted her chin a proud fraction. 'Who he was is not important,' she said stiffly. 'I haven't seen him since I left Hobson's, and...'

'But you'd like to?' Sloan questioned, sounding tough.

'No!' Whitney denied sharply. She recalled angrily that only after she had known she loved Dermot had she found out more about him, and she turned her anger on Sloan, telling him, 'I discovered too late that he was married, and was still living with his wife and family. How could I want to see a man like that when, aside from any other consideration, I knew the hurt my father caused my mother when she learned that for years he had been betraying her and had been having an affair with another woman?'

Oh, God! Whitney thought as her anger fizzled out. What is it about this man that has me telling him my innermost secrets? She flicked a glance at him, but she could read none of what he was thinking from his cool expression.

'You left your job at Hobson's because of him, of course?' he questioned, his voice as cool as his look.

'Of course,' Whitney replied, with a good degree of frost in her own voice.

'How long have you been with your present firm?' Sloan wanted to learn.

'I haven't seen Dermot for nearly four months, if that's what you want to know!' Whitney flared, and could have cut out her tongue. He had her doing it again! Not only had she given Sloan a fair idea of how long she had been with Alford Plastics, but she had also told him the first name of the man she loved!

'So how does young Keston feature in your scheme of things?' Sloan asked, sounding tough again.

Whitney had, by then, formed the view that one Mr Sloan Illingworth was a bit too much! But now that she had told him about her disaster of a romance with Dermot, her pride alone decreed that Sloan should not be left under any illusion that she was pining for her married love.

'Toby,' she said in measured tones, 'has, in the short time I've known him, become a very dear friend. So much so,' she went on to stretch the truth somewhat, 'that we now go practically everywhere together.' Peeping up at Sloan from beneath her long lashes, she saw that he was looking fairly grim. Good, she thought, I hope I'm boring him to death. 'Which is why,' she thought to bore him some more, 'it was natural that Toby should ask me to partner him when he had an invitation to a party at your house.'

'And which is why,' Sloan said sourly, 'since you go practically everywhere together, he naturally forgot to take you back with him when the party broke up.'

Swine! she fumed silently. She had forgotten that Toby, in no condition to remember anything that night, had been driven away from the party by his sister—Valerie, too, conveniently forgetting her.

Railing against Sloan Illingworth as she silently did while the waiter served their final course, all at once Whitney realised why it was that Sloan was so sour with her. And suddenly all anger and rebellion against him deserted her. The evening had started off far more pleasantly than the way they had parted the last time she had seen him, she realised. So it must have been in his mind to make the evening as enjoyable as he could before he got to the crux of why they were here—hadn't Mrs Orton said he was a kind man? But, the waiter now having gone from their table, and with talk of that disastrous party still in the air, Whitney was conscious that the time had come for him to open a painful wound and enlist her aid with regard to him getting back together again with the woman he loved.

'Have you seen Miss Caufield recently?' Whitney thought to bring the matter out into the air as a start to him discussing what he had to with her.

'No,' he said shortly, and looked as though to say, what the devil did she think it had to do with her whom he saw, or whom he didn't see, for that matter?

But Whitney had been along the same avenue of hurt pride herself, so she was not at all offended but as ready and as willing as ever to go and see Gleda, or to do whatever else he thought she could do to help. Though unless he soon told her what it was he wanted of her, Whitney thought that he would never get back together with his ex-fiancée.

'Look, Sloan,' she said softly, realising that perhaps she should have called him Mr Illingworth, but it was too late now, 'I'm here with you now because I want to do everything I can to help.' She saw his small start of surprise at her willingness, but she smiled and pressed on. 'So won't you tell me why you wanted to see me, and what...'

'Why can't I have wanted to see you purely because I wanted to see you again?' he cut in coolly.

Beating down an absurd little flurry which his words had created inside of her, Whitney knew at that point that Sloan must be one of the proudest of men. For, while he must be desperate to get back with Gleda, Whitney suspected that it was against his creed to ask a favour of anyone.

'Because I've a feeling you never do anything without a reason,' she answered his question. 'And, since *my* reason for being here is because—being the culprit responsible for Gleda walking out on your engagement— I want to help all I can to re-unite you, I just know the only reason *you* asked me to dine was because of her.'

For a long time after she had finished speaking, Sloan just sat looking at her. Whitney did not know for sure what he was thinking, but she had a pretty shrewd idea that he was glad she had not misinterpreted the reasons behind his invitation out. Although it seemed an age before he at last admitted it.

'You're—right, of course,' he owned, with a rueful smile. 'I did want to see you for reasons which are— hmm—a little different, perhaps, from normal.'

'Gleda...' Whitney stepped in to prompt, ever ready to help him out.

Sloan's shaking his head threw her somewhat. Though she was more staggered than thrown when he finally came clean, and told her, 'Not Gleda.' And while Whitney stared at him, he told her solemnly, 'I've had to accept that my ex-fiancée and I will never be anything to each other now, and...'

'But,' she started to protest, 'you have to be! You belong to each other! If I hadn't happened to be in your bed just at that particular moment, you and she would still be engaged!'

Sloan shrugged—manfully, Whitney thought. 'Whatever,' he said, and went on, 'Believe me when I tell you that I know that Gleda Caufield and I will never marry.'

'But...' Whitney tried again to protest, only, as if she had not spoken, Sloan was going on,

'However, with the stark fact being that I no longer have a fiancée, I have a—a more immediate concern.'

'You—have?' she questioned on a gasp.

Sloan nodded, and seemed to hesitate, and then, very quietly, he said, 'My—mother.'

'Your mother!' Whitney exclaimed, her eyes shooting wide.

Again he nodded as he told her, 'My mother was so overjoyed when I told her of my engagement that I just— dare not—tell her it's broken.'

Having formed the view that there was little which Sloan would not dare, Whitney sat stunned for a second. 'You mean that your mother has really taken to Gleda and will be...'

'In actual fact,' Sloan broke in, 'the two have never met. But my mother has waited so long for a daughter that she went a little over the top when I broke the news of my engagement to her.'

'Did she?' Whitney murmured faintly.

'She did,' he answered, and went on, 'The thing is, Whitney, that the day after my return to England, my mother was—involved in a—traffic accident, and...'

'Oh, I'm so sorry,' Whitney breathed, realising from the hesitant way he had spoken that it upset him to talk about it. And, remembering her own mother being involved in a traffic accident, she began fearfully, 'Is she...'

'She's recovering from her—physical injuries,' he told her quickly. 'But, since only I know how much it will upset her to hear that I'm no longer engaged, I—just can't tell her. Not yet.'

'Of course you can't,' Whitney said stoutly, her heart going out not only to Sloan, who through her fault entirely and not his—was no longer engaged to be married, but also to his poor mother.

Suddenly, though, through her emotional sensitivity, Whitney realised that she had no earthly idea why Sloan had asked her to dine with him. He had admitted he had wanted to see her for reasons that were a little different from normal. But if he had accepted that his engagement was irretrievably broken, and it therefore followed that he did not want her help in getting back with

Gleda, what other possible reason, for goodness' sake, could he have?

'Sloan,' she said slowly, and she saw that he was looking at no one but her, 'why, may I ask, did you invite me to eat with you tonight?'

For long moments he stared levelly at her, and then, suddenly, he replied, 'I need a fiancée to present to my mother when she's discharged from hospital. Since through you I've lost the only legitimate fiancée I've had, I propose, Whitney, that you shall take her place.'

CHAPTER FOUR

TIME and again on Saturday morning Whitney wished that she had never uttered that phrase which had included the words, 'if there's anything I can do...' She hated deception of any kind, and yet here she was having agreed to deceive Sloan's mother into believing that she was his fiancée!

Whitney tried to immerse herself in her chores, but she found, even as she gave her already tidy flat a thorough 'going over', that physical work in no way stopped the brain from thinking.

Again she wondered how she could ever have agreed to Sloan Illingworth's preposterous suggestion! But wondering about it did not make it go away. It was a fact that she *had* agreed that, once his sick mother was out of hospital, she was going to deceive the poor woman.

Whitney sighed. Reliving the events of the previous evening, she didn't see that she could have done anything else but agree to deceive her. For it seemed that since her accident Mrs Illingworth had been in a constant state of anxiety about her son. As Sloan had explained, to tell her now of his broken engagement could do his parent only harm, because she would then start fretting about his broken heart.

Recalling how her head had jerked up at that last bit, Whitney also recalled how manfully Sloan was covering up the fact that he was bleeding inside. She had felt awash with guilt that, through her, he was suffering. 'Oh,

Sloan...' she had said apologetically, and it had been then that he had, figuratively speaking, twisted her arm by reminding her of her 'if there's anything I can do...' offer.

'Yes, but I meant in relation to Gleda...' she had tried to protest.

'And what would you call this, if not in relation to her?' he had demanded.

Whitney polished furniture and plumped up already plumped-up cushions, and railed impotently against her fate. Oh, if only Mrs Illingworth had met Gleda Caufield, then this farcical scheme of Sloan's would never be able to get off the ground. As it was, his poor, frail mother was not yet well enough to cope with the introduction of a real fiancée, let alone a mock one.

Sloan had not explained why his mother and fiancée had never met, so Whitney could only assume that the engagement must have happened shortly before he had left England to do his three-month spell of globe-trotting. Quite obviously there had been no mutually convenient time for all three to meet; time only for Sloan to acquaint his parent with the joyous news that her long wait for a daughter was coming to an end.

She was already sensitive to his mother's feelings, or any mother's feelings for that matter, and Whitney sighed again as, committed to go through with it, she wondered why Sloan had thought it necessary to take her out to dinner last night? He could just as easily have told her what he had to, perhaps if not over the phone, then in the comfort of her flat. That was, she thought sourly, unless he had wanted to check first that she didn't eat her peas with her knife before he voiced his outrageous plan to introduce her to his mother as his fiancée.

With the knowledge hanging over her that Sloan Illingworth would be in touch again when his mother was well enough to meet her, Whitney grew fed up with herself and with the thoughts that chased around in her head. Putting away her cleaning materials, she rinsed her hands and went upstairs to seek out Erica.

'If you're studying, I'm not staying,' she told her when Erica came to the door.

'Crumbs—those beans I borrowed from you last week!' Erica exclaimed. 'I forgot all about them,' she added, and went on, 'I'm not studying, and providing you haven't come on a bean hunt and will turn a blind eye to the clutter—I only clean up when there's an ''R'' in the month——' she quipped '—then come in and have a cup of coffee while I tell you my news.'

Whitney laughed and went in. Erica was just the tonic she needed. 'So, I'm sitting comfortably,' Whitney told her when Erica had cleared a space at the kitchen table and removed a pile of books from the other kitchen chair, and they both sat drinking coffee.

'Guess what?' Erica beamed, unable to hold it in any longer. 'I'm an aunt!'

'Nikki?' Whitney questioned, aware that Erica's much-loved younger sister who lived in the Midlands had been about to produce.

'I had a phone call five minutes ago. Isn't it great?' she exclaimed. 'Mother and son both well, although the poor little perisher's been blighted with Eric for his middle name.'

'Why, that's lovely!' Whitney told her.

'The sentiment is,' Erica agreed, finding a sudden urgent need to blow her nose. The emotional moment over, however, they talked for many minutes on the new arrival, James Eric, when Erica then announced her other piece of news—there was a new man in her life. 'Though when I'll have the time to see him, lord alone knows,' she said, and was talking of killing two birds with one stone by getting him to take her to see the new baby, which couldn't possibly wait beyond next weekend, then she suddenly said, 'I'm hogging it all—what's new with you?'

'I—er—went out to dinner last night with—Sloan Illingworth,' Whitney confessed.

'Sloan Illingworth!' Erica exclaimed with widening eyes. 'Isn't he the man you were found in bed...'

'The same,' Whitney said quickly.

When she returned to her flat, confusion had replaced the depression she had felt when she had gone up to see Erica. For as she had told Erica where Sloan had taken her, and the ins and outs of what she had eaten, Whitney had discovered in herself an utmost reluctance to tell her friend—who was the soul of discretion—anything at all about Sloan's proposal that she play the part of his fiancée. And if the fact that for once she had held back from confiding everything in Erica was not sufficient to make her wonder *what* had held her back, Whitney had more to wonder at when she realised something else: that as she had told Erica the parts she had, it had come to her that she had found Sloan Illingworth's company not only stimulating, but—yes—enjoyable.

Puzzled as to why she should find his company stimulating and enjoyable when she wasn't even certain she liked the man, Whitney suddenly remembered that she had invited Toby to dinner that night. 'Oh, help!' she breathed, and, catching hold of her purse and her shopping basket, she hared round to the shops for something for the evening meal.

By Monday she was on more of an even keel. The dinner with Toby had passed without incident and, nice person that he was, without him overstaying his welcome. That her Sunday was spent with her thoughts still more on her Friday evening dinner companion than her Saturday evening one was no mystery to her. Especially when, as Sunday evening approached, she came to the realisation that it was not that she found Sloan's company so stimulating and enjoyable at all. It was just that his proposition that she pretend to be his fiancée was such a mind-blower that it had left no room in her head for her to think and fret over Dermot. For the first time since she and Dermot had split, something had happened which had left little space in her head to think painful thoughts of him.

By the end of that week, though, thoughts of Dermot and the deceit he had practised in not telling her that he was married had crept back to mingle in with her thoughts on the deceit she was going to practise on Sloan's mother—when Sloan's mother was well enough.

Whitney made her way home from her office on Friday aware that Mrs Illingworth must still be very poorly in hospital, because she had thought that Sloan might ring her, but not so much as a peep had she heard out of him.

Thoughts of Sloan and how he was probably spending a lot of his time visiting his mother in hospital occupied Whitney during the evening. When she wasn't thinking of Sloan, she was thinking of Dermot, neither subject doing very much to cheer her up.

At eleven o'clock she decided to go to bed and forget about the pair of them. At five-past eleven Erica galloped down to her flat and knocked her usual tattoo on her door.

'Just remembered,' she panted, the pencil sticking out from the top-knot style of her hair denoting that she was in the middle of studying, 'have you got a decent suitcase I can borrow?'

'Come in,' Whitney invited, and was, as ever, cheered by Erica, who breezed in behind her declaring that her suitcase was 'the end' and that since Chris—her new man-friend—came from a fifty-pound-note class of family, and was driving her to stay overnight at her sister's home, she didn't want to put the poor bloke off should he offer to carry her falling-apart luggage.

'Can't stop,' she said in a rush when, handing over her best suitcase, Whitney asked her if she'd got time for a warm drink. 'Chris is one of those punctual types, so I'd better pack tonight when I've finished my homework.'

Whitney went out with Toby on Saturday, and she spent a quiet day on her own on Sunday. She was glad to get to work on Monday, but she began to think, as each day followed the next, that Sloan Illingworth's statement that she must pretend to be his fiancée must have been some figment of her imagination! For another Friday morning had arrived, and she had not heard another word from him.

It was two weeks that night since she had dined with him, and he had startled her by what he had said, she mused as she took the cover off her typewriter. She breathed a sigh of relief as she sat down at her desk. By the look of it, she was not going to be called upon to deceive Sloan's mother. She had no way of knowing what had happened to make him change his mind about wanting her to act the part of his fiancée, but quite clearly *something* had. It was not outside the realms of possibility that he and Gleda had made it up, of course.

Whitney's brow wrinkled; oddly, she found that last thought displeasing.

She had just returned from getting herself a mid-morning cup of coffee when, answering her phone, she was made aware that her sigh of relief had been a mite premature.

'You'd better let me have your home phone number,' Sloan Illingworth snarled in her ear.

The shock of hearing him, as much as his disagreeable tone, caused Whitney to trot out her phone number before she could think. 'How's...' she began to follow up to ask how his mother was, but, for the second time when talking to him on the phone, she found that she was talking to the air. A flare of anger exploded in her. 'Damn him,' she fumed, and slammed the phone back on its rest.

Sorely wishing that she had told him to get lost when he had asked for her home phone number, Whitney took some minutes to simmer down. Who did he think he was to call her up and then, before she had time to think, snarl at her the way he had? Just because he didn't want to discuss any of the vile scheme he had in mind over his office phone, he...

Whitney began to calm down when she started to see that perhaps his scheme was not so vile. Perhaps it was more merely a necessity in this instance, with him wanting to do what he could to ensure that his mother made a speedy full recovery.

Having got over her annoyance with him, Whitney left her place of employment that day aware, if she was aware of nothing else, that there seemed every chance that one day soon she would pick up her phone at home and find Sloan Illingworth on the other end.

The weekend passed without her taking a call from him, although she did not stay in all the weekend just on the off-chance. It was Monday evening before the phone in her flat chirruped for attention, however, and her heart started to beat erratically as she went to answer it. Nerves, she realised, were getting to her, for every instinct was telling her whose voice she was likely to hear.

'Hello,' she said when, after taking a few moments, she lifted the receiver.

'Where were you last night?' Sloan Illingworth barked in her ear for her pains.

'Out—on a date!' Whitney, on the instant incensed by his words and his tone, slammed back at him. She was even more incensed by his reply.

'From now on you can forget about your boyfriend, or about dating any other man-friend in the near future!' he rapped. 'From...'

'Like blazes I will!' Whitney flew. 'Who the devil do you think you are? I'll date any man I please! I'll...'

'Not while you're engaged to me, you won't,' he grated.

'I don't happen to be engaged to...'

'For the purposes of my mother's peace of mind, you are,' he cut in toughly.

Silenced for a brief while, her sting drawn at being reminded that, for his mother's sake, she had agreed to pretend to be engaged to him, Whitney collected herself to ask, as evenly as she could, 'H-how is your mother?'

'Fair,' he said, when he too had paused as if to collect himself. 'With luck,' he then went on, 'she'll shortly be out of hospital and coming to Heathlands to convalesce. Which means that you and I have some ground-work to put in.'

'Ground-work?' Whitney questioned.

'Of course,' he said shortly. 'Of necessity, you and I will have to go around together...'

'Why in the world should we do that?' she asked heatedly, her pride up in arms by his 'of necessity'. No man *had* to take her *anywhere* of necessity!

'For God's sake!' Sloan roared, as if he too had taken exception, in his case to the fact that she clearly did not want to go out with him. 'My mother may be a shade—confused—at the moment, but she certainly isn't dim. She'll guess straight away that our engagement is nothing but a sham—with retrograde consequences for her—if neither you nor I can freely talk of the various places we've been together.'

'But...' Whitney started to protest, only to find that Sloan's saying that his mother was a shade confused was sapping her will to argue the matter. 'But... what about my boyfriend?' Trying desperately hard to find some good reason to make him see why she shouldn't go out with him, Whitney realised that her panic was making her as deceitful as the next. Because by no stretch of the imagination could Toby be called her 'boyfriend' in the accepted use of the term. 'What about him?' she ploughed on. 'He's not going to be very thrilled when I have to tell him I can't see him because I'm seeing you.'

'He'll be far less thrilled,' Sloan rapped back, sounding tough again, 'should he get to hear how my engagement came to an abrupt end when my fiancée found you in bed with me!'

'You—*pig*!' Whitney yelled down the phone.

'Love you too, sweetheart!' Sloan snarled, and had only one thing to say before he rang off. 'We're going to the theatre tomorrow. Be ready!'

Whitney was fuming when the phone went dead in her ear. One of these days she was going to beat him to it, she'd be hanged if she didn't! Furious with him that he should dare to threaten to blackmail her, for that was what his statement was all about, Whitney replaced her own receiver. 'Pig' was too good a name for him, she thought irately, having not taken kindly to his intimation that he would have a word in Toby's ear if she didn't go along with him. Sloan plainly knew, or had somehow deducted, that Toby was completely unaware of how the party had ended that night.

For the next half-hour, Whitney silently raged against Sloan Illingworth. Slowly, then, she began to cool down. And it was then that she began to wonder why the dickens she had panicked at the thought of going places with him. Why, too, had she tried to make out that Toby was more a boyfriend than just the friend that he was? It was a riddle to her.

Going over her panic of that time again, however, Whitney was startled when it dawned on her that the thought of going places with Sloan had made her feel vulnerable! Vulnerable, she realised, and a little afraid.

But afraid of what? When the answer came back 'afraid of being hurt again', Whitney threw her theorising out of the window. She still loved Dermot, so how could going out with Sloan Illingworth hurt her? It couldn't hurt her a scrap, she resolved, not if she went out with him a hundred times it couldn't.

Whitney spent a restless night with one thought after another going through her head. She left her bed the following morning having admitted that maybe there was some truth in his statement that his mother was never going to believe that they were engaged if, during any conversation, they could only talk of the one single, solitary dinner-date they had shared.

She went to her office knowing that, for his mother's sake, and his mother's sake only, she would go out with him. But she came home from her office not liking him any better for thinking he could blackmail her into going out with him because of her fear of what he might tell Toby.

Sloan had not said what time he would call for her, and Whitney was too much against him to ring him and ask. But, to prove that she was unafraid to go out with him, she was ready in good time.

She had thought she had herself on quite an even keel as she waited for her bell at the front door to ring. But when her bell did sound, she was so jumpy that she leapt about a foot. Taking up her handbag, she secured her flat, and went to start a travesty for which she had little taste.

However, since she was most assuredly definite about her inner distaste for the whole business, she wondered at that part of her that felt a most peculiar thrill when, as she greeted Sloan on the top doorstep, he towered over her, and said civilly, 'You look charming, Whitney.'

Dearly wishing to answer with a trite, 'it's just something I threw on'—which wasn't strictly true, for, appetite for the evening or no, she had still deliberated for some time on what to wear—she settled for a cool, 'Thank you.'

Sloan went down the steps with her, and once in his car they were soon away. But though she was determined to stay cool with him, Whitney could not deny another flutter of something which felt closely akin to pride at being escorted by him when, leaving his car, she walked with him the short way to the theatre.

'I hope you like mysteries,' he murmured when they were seated.

'I prefer them to farce,' she told him coldly, and turned to face the front—though not before she saw a small movement at the corners of his mouth as though he had found her barb amusing but was trying hard to hold back a grin.

Fortunately, just then the play started. It was a good play with fine actors, and Whitney was inclined to enjoy the performance, but she was finding that she was having something of a job to forget about the man by her side.

During the interval they left their seats to stretch their legs and take some refreshment. Nothing if not well brought up, Whitney answered any remark which Sloan chose to make with the good manners of her up-bringing, but otherwise she retained her cool exterior.

Her cool attitude was still with her when they left the theatre and walked back to Sloan's car. So, too, did her good manners stand up to the test. For as they sat in his vehicle and Sloan waited for a gap in the theatre-going traffic so that he could pull out, Whitney used the silence in the car to drop out what she saw as an obligatory courtesy.

'Thank you——' she began unemotionally.

But she was stopped from going any further when, tersely, Sloan cut in, 'The evening isn't over yet!'

'Not over...?' she echoed aloofly, when from his tone she gathered the distinct impression that he was not too enamoured of her cool, if polite, manner—which bothered her not in the slightest.

'That's what I said,' he clipped. 'There's a nightclub...'

'Nightclub!' she exclaimed, forgetting to be cool for a moment in her surprise. Though she was soon draping a mantle of hauteur about her when, having no intention whatsoever of being taken on to a nightclub, she argued frigidly, 'Surely that isn't *completely* necessary.'

Sloan turned his head, and in the well-lit area about them Whitney fancied that she saw chips of ice start to glitter in his eyes. There was no mistaking the fact that she had irritated him, if not angered him, however, when he rapped, 'Perhaps it isn't necessary this evening,' and, lest she thought she could breathe a sigh of relief, threatened, 'We can go to a nightclub some other time.' And, having succeeded in irritating *her*, if not angering her, he took his eyes from her and steered his car into the stream of traffic.

In silence they drove back to her flat, where Whitney could hardly wait to get out of the car. She guessed that he had been brought up somewhere along the same lines as herself when he got out of his car and escorted her to the outside front door.

The surfacing of his good manners made her aware that, annoyed with her as he undoubtedly had been a short while ago, he now seemed to be doing his best to retrieve the situation. 'Allow me,' he said pleasantly, and, taking the front door key from her hand, he unlocked the door and pushed it inwards. Finding the light switch, he flicked on the hall light, and handed her back her key.

'Thank you,' she said with equal pleasantness and, the evening over as far as she was concerned, she stepped over the doorway and had a 'goodnight' ready on her lips as she turned to close the door on her escort. It didn't quite work out like that. For one thing, when she turned Sloan was standing in the doorway, which made it impossible for her to close the door until he had stepped back.

She looked at him in enquiry, but she did not trust at all the smile that was suddenly there on his face when, with some considerable charm, he suggested, 'For the sake of authenticity in our engagement, do you not think that perhaps I should see the inside of your flat?'

What Whitney thought just then might have scorched his ears had she said it. She swallowed the words down but, forgetting that he had not long ago used the self-same words, in her search for something fairly polite, she sent him a cool, 'Some other time.'

Sloan looked at her and did not seem at all put out, which niggled her some more. She was further niggled, not to say fuming when, with a murmured, 'Now you really are playing the game my way', he even had the cheek to smile. 'Goodnight, Whitney,' he said, quite audaciously she thought, and, stepping back, he returned to his car.

But for waking the household, Whitney would have slammed the door violently shut after him. But since that option was not permissible she closed the door and went seething up to her flat, realising that, for all her antagonistic feelings to him she had just as good as agreed to go out with him again!

Whitney made short work of her ablutions that night. Inside half an hour she was washed and in her night attire and was lying in her bed. Wretched, cursed man, she chafed.

Oddly, though, as sleep came to claim her, her crossness with Sloan started to disappear. She was still thinking of him and his impudent parting smile when, with a smile picking at the corners of her own mouth, she fell asleep.

CHAPTER FIVE

WHITNEY was deep in thought as she wondered one
Saturday afternoon just how—or when, for that matter—
had she grown to like Sloan Illingworth.

Casting her mind back, she reflected how she had gone
out with him many times since that night just over a
month ago when he had first taken her to the theatre.
She had objected that night, she recalled, to his as-
sumption that she was willing to go on to a nightclub,
but she had been to a nightclub with him since, and, it
had to be admitted, she had enjoyed the experience.

In fact, she mused, she could not say with any truth
that she had disliked any of the places she had been to
with him. She had been determined from the outset that,
if go out with him she must, she was not going to be
the most affable of companions. So how was it that she
should have done a complete turn-around to have become
exactly that?

Catching herself smiling, Whitney straightened her
expression, but only to realise, with something of a
shock, that she smiled more frequently just lately! And
another thing that shook her was that, when she tried
to analyse what it was about life that made it seem so
pleasant to her, she suddenly realised that thoughts of
Dermot were not so constantly in her mind as they had
been.

Which, she thought a moment later, was not so sur-
prising, because she just didn't have so much time for

any in-depth thinking of late. Sloan, of course, and her outings with him, were the reason for that.

Her thoughts latched on to her third date with him. He had telephoned her at her flat the night after he had taken her to the theatre. 'Fancy joining me for dinner tomorrow?' he'd queried smoothly.

With his mother so sick, and with no Gleda Caufield sprinting back to his arms, Whitney hadn't seen what chance she had of refusing. 'There's nothing I'd like better,' she had told him sarcastically.

'I knew deep down you liked me,' Sloan replied, and she'd wanted to hit him for taking her sarcasm as sincerity.

Again he had put the phone down before she could say another word, but, on thinking about it, Whitney had had to smile. Because if there was one thing Sloan Illingworth wasn't, it was stupid. He had known *darn well* that she was being sarcastic.

She pondered that perhaps that had been the start of her beginning to genuinely like him? At all events, she had lost some of her cool, starchy manner when he'd come to take her out to dinner the following evening.

'Did anyone ever tell you that you have the most sensational pair of green eyes?' he'd said, when he had taken her home after a superb meal.

Whitney had taken the key from him after he had opened the front door, and had switched on the hall light. 'All the time,' she had said solemnly and, on purpose, she had made her green eyes huge. She had seen that a grin was tugging at the corners of his mouth. 'Goodnight,' she'd said quickly, and he had stepped back.

'Goodnight, Whitney,' he'd replied quietly.

She had gone out with him again on the following Saturday. That was the night he had taken her to a nightclub. That was the night, she recalled, when she had found out a little more about his likes and dislikes. As he in turn had found out more about her, she realised, because he was a dab hand at the third degree and never seemed to run short of questions. Notwithstanding that, she reflected, she herself had discovered that they had many likes and dislikes in common.

A few days had passed then without her seeing or hearing from Sloan, but she knew that he would be in touch. His mother, and her well-being, meant too much to him for it not to be so.

Realising that, together with being a very busy man, he was having to make as much spare time as he could in order to fit in plenty of hospital visiting, Whitney had taken the opportunity of having no date with Sloan to go out with Toby. In her book, it just wasn't polite to take up with one man and to drop the other cold. For, on the face of it, Toby was more her friend than Sloan was.

'Can you make an art gallery opening this evening?' Sloan had rung up to ask when five days had gone by without a word from him.

'For you, anything,' she had answered sourly, and had been immediately aghast that she had sounded for all the world as though she was peeved that it had taken him so long to get in touch! 'What time?' she had asked quickly and, having being told the time that Sloan would call for her, she came away from the phone wondering at her initial reaction to him. Good grief! Quickly she reminded herself—when, strictly speaking, no reminder should have been necessary—that the only reason Sloan was asking her to accompany him on these various outings was in the interests of authenticity. Her only reason for agreeing to go out with him was, since she had been instrumental in his engagement's ending, for his poor mother's sake.

Having re-established that fact, Whitney had got ready to go out with Sloan that evening knowing for certain that she was not remotely interested in him. She was still feeling bruised from her experience with Dermot, and she knew that it would be a very long time before she took an interest in any male. She did not even want Sloan for a friend.

Despite her mental assertions that she did not want so much as friendship with Sloan, it was that same evening that their relationship, of necessity, took a friendlier turn...

The paintings on display at the art gallery were divided mainly between landscapes and domestic scenes. But, having looked their fill at each picture in succession and then moved on, they came to a section which could only be described as 'way-out' art.

For about thirty seconds Whitney stood with Sloan as they peered into the depths of the navy-, orange- and red-daubed canvas. Then she studied the catalogue which Sloan had given her and, reading that the exhibit was entitled 'Mirth', her eyes went back to the painting, and suddenly she saw it.

Excited, she turned to Sloan. But one look at his disgusted 'My God!' expression, and she knew that she was alone in her discovery. 'It's lovely!' she exclaimed when, more than ready to move to the next painting, Sloan caught hold of her elbow as though to guide her on.

'What is?' he enquired, halting in his step, but keeping a hold on her elbow.

'Don't you see it?' she asked, directing his gaze back to the picture.

'We're talking of this navy- and orange-plastered abomination masquerading under the name of art?' he enquired and, his mouth curving, he took his eyes away from the picture and looked down into her excited shining green eyes.

'Look again,' she urged him. 'Look at the red; it's a mouth, a red, laughing mouth.' Owning that at first she had thought the picture 'weird', Whitney was now much taken with it. 'Well, I like it,' she told him as they moved on.

'And I,' Sloan smiled as they stopped at the next canvas, his eyes going from her eyes to her sweet mouth, 'rather think I like you.'

There was no answer to that, Whitney discovered. But as her heart gave the most crazy flutter, 'Keep your mind on the art work,' she told him repressively, and suddenly they were both grinning.

Her heartbeats had long settled down to normal when Sloan drove her home, but something perhaps a shade warmer had been added to the acquaintanceship. At any rate, she felt that she could speak more freely, and without risk of offending him.

Realising that his mother must still be in hospital or he would by now have made the suggestion that she come and see his mother at Heathlands, they were nearly back at Whitney's flat, when she said, 'Is your mother any better, Sloan?'

'She's—about the same,' he answered, and he seemed just then to need to give all of his concentration to his driving.

Whitney left it for a few minutes, but she thought that she had some rights too, even if she was getting the blame that Sloan was no longer engaged. When she thought that enough time had elapsed she tentatively reminded him, 'You—er—mentioned once that your mother was a little—confused.'

'Did I?' he queried, and seemed surprised that he had ever told her anything so personal about his mother.

'Has her confusion cleared at all?' Whitney persisted, if gently. 'I mean, I know,' she said understandingly, 'that sometimes when people are getting on in years...' She broke off. She had no idea how old Sloan's mother was, but if she'd had him late in life she could be well over seventy by now. And while she knew that seventy was no age at all these days, Mrs Illingworth had been in a serious motor accident and might well have suffered a knock on her head into the bargain.

'The last time I spoke to her she—er—seemed very far away,' Sloan told her as if it was being dragged out of him.

'Oh, I'm so sorry,' Whitney murmured in full sympathy, her heart going out to the poor lady as a memory flooded in of how very far away her mother had been in her thoughts before her death. When Sloan seemed reluctant to add anything to what he'd said, though, Whitney decided not to question him any more.

So he had taken her home and, feeling sensitive to him, she had invited him up for a cup of coffee, but he had declined, saying that he'd some work to do when he got home. Whitney had again realised how busy he must be, and she would not have been surprised if another five days had gone by without a word from him. But, the very next day he had telephoned, and they had gone out to dinner.

They had, after that, been frequent companions, but always Sloan had taken her to different places. All, she knew, with the aim in due time of them both being able to talk with his mother at length on the various things they had done together. The fact that his mother must still be in hospital showed Whitney that the accident must have been serious indeed. For, to her certain knowledge, she'd heard of people having all manner of major surgery, and yet being discharged from hospital inside two or three weeks.

As time went on she thought that perhaps Sloan might suggest taking her to the hospital and introducing her there as his fiancée to his mother. But when he did no such thing, she could only assume that his parent was still being troubled by confusion, and that Sloan still considered it better to leave introductions until she was well enough to be recuperating at Heathlands...

Whitney came out of her reverie that Saturday and wondered if she would see anything of Sloan this weekend. The last time she had seen him was Thursday, but he had been flying off early on Friday for some business meeting he had scheduled in Switzerland, and might not be back until some time on Sunday.

Going to make herself a cup of tea, Whitney suddenly found it most odd that it should have been Sloan who had occupied her thoughts for the last half-hour, and not Dermot. Perhaps it wasn't so odd after all, though, because it was fairly recently that she had seen Sloan, and months since she had seen Dermot.

Taking her tray of tea back with her into her sitting-room, Whitney found she was wondering if Sloan still thought constantly about Gleda. Her name was never mentioned between them, so if it still hurt that she would have nothing more to do with him, he was keeping it to himself. But... Whitney's thoughts broke off when the pattern of Erica's familiar knock sounded on the woodwork of the flat door.

'You smelled the teapot,' Whitney accused with a smile as she invited her in.

'Can't stop, really can't,' Erica panted. 'I'm having one of those days where I should have started at three o'clock this morning to get it all crammed in. I've just remembered, though—you know I told you that I'm being a godmother at James Eric's christening tomorrow—well,' she took a hurried breath, 'I've just realised, since this is serious stuff, that I haven't got a hat I can wear. You haven't got one I could borrow, have you?'

'I've got a couple, I think,' Whitney told her, and was just about to invite her into her bedroom to have a trying-on session when the bell to her flat rang. Whitney's heart acted in the most peculiar fashion when her initial thought was that Sloan, home before he had thought he would be, had called to see her. How ridiculous, she thought a split second later; not only was Sloan still miles away in Switzerland, but he wouldn't call without first telephoning anyway. 'If you can hang on while I go and see who that is,' she quickly told Erica, 'I'll...' Erica, hopping from one foot to the other, told her that she hadn't got a minute to waste.

'Do you mind if I come back later?' she asked. 'Every moment counts with me today.'

Whitney parted from Erica on the landing, Erica to go up, she to go down. With no idea of who her caller could be, Whitney pulled open the front door, to be confronted by Toby who, she immediately saw, was not his usual smiling self.

'I thought you weren't in!' he exclaimed, and, as a trace of guilt smote Whitney that she'd had to turn down several invitations recently, she smiled a welcome at him.

'I was just having a cup of tea,' she told him. 'Are you coming up for one?'

'I should like to,' he accepted, but she thought he was strangely quiet as he traipsed up the stairs with her.

'So,' she encouraged him when, with a cup and saucer placed on a table near him, she sat sipping from her own cup of tea, 'what brings you to this neck of the woods?'

'Er—you, actually,' he said, somewhat diffidently.

'Er—how do you mean?' she asked, and suddenly she began to feel wary.

'Well,' he said, and then seemed to be at a loss to know how best to go on. 'Damn,' he swore mildly. 'You'd never know that I practised all morning what I was going to say to you. But now, seeing you, being with you, it's—all gone.'

Whitney was not sure that she liked the sound of this, but she had grown fond of Toby, and if she could help him out, she would.

'What do you want to say to me that needs so much practising, Toby?' she asked him quietly.

'I—can't...' he began, and then followed it up with, 'At first, I was going to write to you. Then—well, then, I knew that I just couldn't wait to hear what you'd say in answer. I just couldn't bear it if you'd decided to post your reply back—it could be ages before I knew if you cared for me the way that I care for you.' Suddenly, he stopped, looked amazed, and said disbelievingly, 'I've just said it! I've just told you that I care for you! That's what I wanted to...' He broke off when he saw that his joy that he'd got the words out was not exactly mirrored in the expression which Whitney wore. 'You don't care for me...' he began, but Whitney started to recover from his most unexpected declaration—if declaration it was.

'I'm not sure quite what you're saying, Toby,' she interrupted him quickly, finding that she had the utmost difficulty in believing that he was seriously declaring his love for her. 'I told you before I ever went out with you,' she as quickly added, 'that I . . .'

'I know,' he butted in, taking a gulp of breath. 'You were "off" men then, you told me, so I realised that someone had hurt you. Which is why,' he said on another gulp, 'I haven't rushed you or—or said anything. Only, with you now going out with someone else, as well as me, I sort of took it that you're not so "off" men as you once were, and, well, to be honest, I sort of got scared that he might propose to you before I did.'

Propose! Whitney was aghast at the words that had left Toby in such a torrent, and she just did not know how to cope with it. Plainly Toby had put two and two together and had deduced, when she had turned down some of his invitations, that she was seeing someone else. But, having loved, and having been hurt by love herself, she hated the thought of having to hurt him.

'Oh, Toby—Toby,' she said helplessly.

But it seemed that he had read all the answer he needed in her unhappy look. 'You don't—care for me,' he said dully.

'As a friend, I care for you,' she told him sorrowfully, 'But Toby, only as a friend.'

'I didn't really think I'd got much of chance,' he told her. But, after several moments of wringing her heart with his downcast look, he made great efforts to brighten up, and added, 'I suppose it's quite something that I have you for a friend.' He lifted up his cup and saucer and took a long draught of tea as if he really needed it. Then, as though he was feeling more his old self, the old self he felt more comfortable with, he said, 'You've had something on for the last three Saturdays, Whitney. Do you suppose that a—friend—would be asking too much if he asked to see you one Saturday in four?'

'You shocker!' Whitney exclaimed softly, as she realised with some surprise that when it came to emotional blackmail, Toby was every bit as capable of using it as Sloan.

'Is it too much to ask?' he questioned, his little schoolboy lost expression coming out in full force.

'I . . .' she hesitated. Would it hurt to go out with Toby tonight? With Sloan still in Switzerland . . . Not that she had to keep her Saturday evenings free for him. In all probability he was painting Zurich red with some elegant Swiss female and . . . Suddenly Whitney was experiencing very hostile feelings against Sloan. 'I don't see why not,' she told Toby, and, as Toby's face became wreathed in smiles, she knew that she could not retract her acceptance.

The second Toby had gone on his way, though, Whitney was wondering what in creation had come over her! The absurd thought popped into her head that maybe a spasm of jealousy had been at the back of her accepting Toby's invitation. But the idea that she had felt jealous at the thought of Sloan dating some 'Gleda equivalent' while he was in Switzerland was so ludicrous that Whitney almost laughed out loud.

Instead she set to work on ousting Sloan from her thoughts and concentrating her attention on Toby. In view of his unexpected proposal of marriage, she had to wonder if she was doing Toby any favours by continuing to see him. She couldn't avoid seeing him at work, but . . .

After much deep thought, she came to the conclusion that it would do no harm to see Toby outside working hours. The simple fact was—and she had loved, so she knew—Toby did not love her. Not in the way he thought he did, anyhow. Only recently he had told her how his sister's ultra-sophisticated friends frightened him half to death, so that more often than not he gave his sister, and her flat, a wide berth. Clearly, Whitney considered, Toby wanted love and marriage. And perhaps it wasn't very complimentary to her—though because she felt she really was his friend, she was unoffended—but the truth was that Toby had felt comfortable and unthreatened with her, and had convinced himself that it was love that he felt.

Having puzzled that out to a satisfactory outcome, Whitney considered that she might talk to Toby somewhere along those lines that evening. That settled, she then remembered Erica, and she was about to go rummaging after the couple of hats which she had told her about when suddenly the phone rang. Whitney was not at all sure how she felt when she recognised Sloan's voice.

'You're back?' she questioned, not certain if he was phoning from England or Switzerland.

'My business didn't take as long as I thought,' he replied, and, while she was starting to feel quite good inside that she had been wrong to suppose that he was dating some Swiss lady, he was going on smoothly, 'With fair wind I should be able to make your place for eight; we'll...'

'Hang on a second!' Whitney cut him off, and she started to get angry on two fronts. First, that she was sure that she didn't give a damn how many Swiss ladies he dated! Second, his pure impudence that, now that His High and Mightiness was back in the country, he had loftily assumed that all he had to do was to pick up the phone and she would jump to do his bidding. 'I'm afraid I'm not free tonight,' she told him acidly.

There was a small pause from the other end, then, 'Why?' he snarled toughly.

With the greatest of pleasure, Whitney sweetly told him, 'I already have an engagement for this evening.'

But only to have her breath taken away when he demanded bluntly, 'Who with?'

As if it was any business of his! 'If you must know,' she retorted sharply, her sweet tone soon gone, 'I'm going out with Toby Kes...' She did not get to finish. Before she could blink an eyelid, Sloan's voice came roaring down the line and caused her to break off.

'I'd have thought you'd have more about you than to keep one man's bed warm while going out with another!' he rapped furiously.

It was done. Whitney had told herself that one day she was going to have the pleasure of leaving him to be the one on the other end hanging on to the phone. And that was exactly what she had done. Enraged with him, she hadn't even been aware what she was doing until she had slammed the phone down on him.

The swine! she fumed. The perfect swine! How dared he talk to her like that? Well, that did it! Never, ever was she going to go out with Mr I'll-make-your-place-for-eight Illingworth again. She'd only gone out with him for his mother's sake anyway, and... Oh, bother it, she seethed, and wished that she hadn't thought of Sloan's poor, confused mother.

Stubbornly, Whitney spend the next ten minutes determined that it was no skin off her nose how bewildered Sloan's mother was. She didn't even know the woman, for goodness' sake!

To haunt her, though, Whitney kept getting flashes of memory of her own dear mother, and of her bewilderment when her husband's mistress of many years had called at their home. Whitney recalled the dreadful days that had followed. Her mother's utter trust in her husband had been broken, and, her faith in him shattered, she had gone around in a perpetually stunned and dazed state.

Whitney blinked back tears at her memories of her own poor, confused mother, but the edge had gone from the anger she had felt against Sloan. She attempted to get her fury back when she reflected that he, not missing much, must have noticed that she had a vulnerable spot where mothers were concerned, and that, having witnessed that vulnerability, he hadn't hesitated to put the pressure on. But the more she wanted to be cross with him, the more it seemed that she remembered how, but for her making free use of his bed, Sloan would still have a fiancée, and would not need her to act that part for him.

Recalling that not once had he bleated about *his* feelings in all of this, Whitney was suddenly undecided about what she should do. Not once had he mentioned his pain or the heartbreak he must be feeling. Manfully, he had kept his feelings to himself; the only feelings he had let her know about were his concern for his mother. It was probably that concern, she suddenly realised, which had seen him speeding through his work so that he could get back to England to visit his mother.

With her thoughts once more centred on Sloan's hospitalised parent, Whitney tried one more stab at getting angry with him, but when that failed, she picked up the phone and dialled Toby's number. Toby was going to hate it, she knew, but . . .

'Hello, Toby,' she said quickly as the ringing tone stopped, 'It's...'

'Whitney!' he exclaimed, not waiting for her to announce who she was. 'I've only just walked in from your place; what can I do for you?'

'It's—I'm...' In view of the pleased surprise in his voice, Whitney felt worse than ever about what she was just about to do, and she was having trouble in getting started. She took a hold on herself. 'I'm sorry, Toby, I really am,' she said, and plunged on, 'but I'm afraid I can't make it tonight, after all.'

'You can't...!' Oh, grief, Whitney thought, and she almost told him then to forget that she had phoned, and that she would see him that night as they had planned. Against that, though, there was Sloan—Sloan's mother. 'It's because of what I said this afternoon, isn't it?' Toby, without knowing it, tore her further apart. 'You've had time to think about it, and you've decided that you don't...'

'Toby, Toby,' Whitney cut him off before he could tear her soft heart further to ribbons. 'It's nothing personal to do with you. It's just that something—er—has cropped up, and I can't see you as I said I would. But it's got nothing to do with the—er—friendship you and I share.'

'You still want to be my friend?'

'Have lunch with me on Monday, my treat,' she told him.

'You're on,' he brightened.

Whitney rang off, growing to think that suddenly life had become very complicated. She next found Sloan's telephone number. Before she set about ringing him though, she realised that, as yet, she had the whole evening free and that she was not committed. She also realised that, from the way she had slammed the phone down on him, she was going to have to sink her pride if she did call him. Whitney spent another few moments wondering if she really wanted to spend the evening with Sloan or if she would prefer her own solitary company in her own solitary flat. Oh, drat the man, she suddenly thought angrily, and a few seconds later she was busily dialling Sloan's home number.

It seemed to take light years before the phone was answered, and her hands grew moist, possibly because it wasn't every day that she sank her pride. But, just as she was about to replace the receiver and tell herself, well, she had tried, suddenly it was picked up.

'Illingworth,' Sloan's voice vibrated in her ear, and all at once Whitney was aware that her heart was thundering.

'So...' she said on a cracked note, but she had the coolness she was desperately searching for when she said more firmly, 'So, get your sails hoisted—I'll be ready at eight.' With that, she quietly replaced the receiver.

CHAPTER SIX

WHEN Whitney came away from the phone, her heart-beats had evened out. She was aware that the only reason her heart had thundered when Sloan had answered the phone was that she had been just about to sink her pride. Starting to feel a little foolish that she had telephoned him at all, Whitney then began to get cross, not only with herself, but with Sloan too.

Regretting the day she had ever met him, regretting the day that she had ever said 'yes' to that wretched sur-prise party, she was sorely tempted to ring him and tell him that she wouldn't see him that evening, after all.

Realising that that would make her feel even more foolish, Whitney went to search her wardrobe for some-thing to wear, feeling very near to throwing in the towel and calling off the whole charade. She could never re-member lying to her own mother, and she had no idea how she would cope when confronted by Sloan's. Nor did she know how she would feel when called upon—if not to lie outright—then to go along with his intro-duction of her as his fiancée.

Sighing, Whitney pulled one of her favourite dresses from her wardrobe, and knew the futility of kicking against the situation she was in. The facts, when taken out and examined, left her with no alternative but to go through with it. She *had* gone to that wretched party. She *had* fallen asleep under the top cover of his bed. She *had* awakened to find him not only lying there beside her, but naked beneath the sheets, with it *seeming* as though they were *both* naked beneath the sheets. And, worst of all, it had been his fiancée who had come and discovered them in the bedroom and had put the only construction possible on finding an undressed couple sharing the same bed.

Not sure which was making her cheeks burn, the guilty picture her last thoughts had brought to mind or the memory of Sloan's broad and naked back as he'd stepped from the bed, Whitney shook such images from her and sighed again. Gleda had done the only thing which any red-blooded woman would do in the circumstances—she had broken off her engagement. Which had left Sloan, when he had quite obviously been unable to get Gleda to listen to his explanation, in a very worrying position: that of knowing that his poor mother was going to be even more distressed than she at present was, if he could not introduce his fiancée to her the moment she came out of hospital.

All of which, Whitney thought disgruntledly as she took her bath, meant that she was back to square one. Because no way, through her own thoughtless actions, could she allow any elderly lady to suffer when her son's being engaged appeared to mean so much to her.

Whitney was dressed in a fresh-looking dress of crisp green linen when Sloan came to call for her. But it was soon apparent that he did not like her any more than she liked him just then.

Thank you, yes, I'm glad I took such trouble to look presentable, Whitney thought sourly when, with more of a grunt for a good evening, Sloan returned down the steps from the front door and went to his car.

'Thank you,' she muttered out loud when inbred courtesy saw him open up the passenger door before he went round to the driver's side.

Sitting beside him as he drove along, Whitney was of the view that the whole evening could be spent in silence for all she cared. She certainly wasn't going to be the one to start up a conversation.

Turning her head a little when five minutes of stony silence had stretched and stretched between them, Whitney observed that Sloan was still wearing a tight-lipped expression. A good time was had by all, she thought acidly, and thought that the limit of their conversation—should they be dining somewhere—was going to be 'pass the cruet'. Just then, though, when she was sure that she didn't give a straw about how stern-faced he looked, Whitney suddenly realised that it could be that he'd had bad news about his mother.

'Your mother...' came rocketing from her then, but she slowed down to ask, 'Have you seen her since you got back?'

For long, long moments Whitney thought that the news about his mother must indeed be bad, because it seemed an age before Sloan answered her. She breathed a sigh of relief, though, when he told her in clipped tones 'I've recently spoken with her on the telephone.' Clearly there had been no time for him to pay a visit to the hospital.

Whitney waited for more, but there was not any more. 'Oh, I see,' she mumbled, and knew that he must have rung his mother as soon as his plane had landed. And as Sloan concentrated on his driving Whitney realised that, of course, since his mother must be in some private wing of whatever hospital she was in, it was highly probable that she had a telephone permanently at her bedside. It was highly probable, too, that she was in constant telephone touch with her son.

The restaurant which Sloan took her to followed the usual pattern in that, in the cause of them being able to talk of a stream of places they had been to, this was somewhere else she had not been to with him before. It was a pleasant enough restaurant, but perhaps lacked the character of some of the other places where they had dined. Though, because she had learned by then that Sloan, without shouting about it, was something of a connoisseur of good food and wine, she rather guessed that the expertise of the chef was most likely what had drawn him to reserve a table there.

The table they were shown to was in a secluded alcove designed so that, although it was possible for them to see quite a large portion of the restaurant, they could not be easily seen, or heard, by other diners.

Whitney took her place, and her bleak thoughts were centred on the 'fun' evening it was going to be if the whole of it was spent with nothing but a grim silence emanating from her escort. But she discovered that her thoughts were a little premature. Though she was well into her *poires au Roquefort* starter when Sloan, his tone no more endearing, had something to say.

'Am I supposed to be grateful that you cancelled your date with Keston?' he asked harshly.

Whitney glanced up at him. It hadn't taken too much imagination before to guess that he was on the look-out for a fight, but the aggressive thrust of his chin now as he waited for her answer left nothing whatsoever to the imagination. He *was* on the look-out for a fight—and she was nettled enough by him to see no reason why she should be the one to make peace.

'I would never suppose you to be grateful for *anything*!' she retorted sharply and, although it took some effort, she tried to appear quite calm and unflustered as she returned her attention to her pears stuffed with Roquefort cheese.

Aware of hate-vibes coming at her across the table, Whitney bounced a few of them back and ignored Sloan as best as she was able when the next course followed. She had by then formed the opinion that, since they had visited the restaurant and sampled its fare together, the purpose of the exercise had been achieved and they might as well leave. But then Sloan suddenly snarled, 'No doubt you offered him an alternative!'

Her head jerked up. 'Who?' she asked.

'Keston!' he rapped. 'Since you're hell-bent on keeping him on a string, you'd have to sweeten the pill when you cancelled tonight's date with him by offering to see him some other time.'

Astounded as much by the logical workings of his mind as by his fierce aggression with her, Whitney stared coldly at him. Not for a minute did she think that she was keeping Toby on a string, but she supposed she had to concede that the rest of Sloan's logic was fairly accurate.

'Well?' he grated, clearly annoyed that she had not answered him. 'Are you seeing him again?'

'If you must know,' Whitney flared, annoyed herself at Sloan's aggression, 'we're lunching together on Monday. And no,' she rushed on, the bit well and truly between her teeth, 'in reply to your pig of a remark over the phone, I am not keeping his bed warm while I'm going out with you.'

'Huh!' Sloan grunted, which left her undecided whether she was meant to take it that he didn't believe that for a minute. 'Have you been seeing him the whole time you've been seeing me?' he snarled.

'What if I have?' Whitney tossed back hotly.

'It just so happens that you're engaged to me!' Sloan reminded her fiercely.

'It just so happens,' she hissed, 'that I'm *pretending* to be engaged to you. And only then,' she threw in for good measure, 'when your mother is well enough for you to introduce me!'

Quietly seething, Whitney wished that she had not mentioned his mother. Thinking about Mrs Illingworth, and how poorly she was, was undermining her anger, and Whitney did not want her anger to be undermined. Dictatorial Sloan Illingworth would walk all over her if she let him. So all right, she owed him, but that didn't give him the right to tell her that she could not have other men-friends!

'I'd have thought,' he continued, not letting up, 'that in view of all that has happened, you'd guard very closely against my mother learning that you date other men!'

'Toby is not "other men"!' Whitney flew, trying hard to keep her voice down even though, with their secluded table, and with the general buzz of the other diners' conversations, no one could overhear. 'And your mother isn't...' She broke off, defeated suddenly. For all she knew, Toby could quite well be acquainted with Mrs Illingworth. Who was to say, with the way her luck was running this year, that the long arm of coincidence wouldn't have Toby meeting up with Sloan's mother and discussing in detail his various doings of late? Taking a steadying breath, she began again. 'For your information, Toby and I are just good friends.'

'Spare me!' Sloan uttered in disgust.

'We are!' Whitney said heatedly. 'We...'

'You'll be telling me next that he's never held your hand!'

'Well, no, but...'

'You'll be telling me next that he's never so much as kissed you!'

Whitney recalled that one kiss of Toby's which had landed on her cheek. 'Well, yes, he has,' she had to own, put off by the dark, scowling expression on Sloan's face. 'But . . .'

'So who the hell are you trying to kid?' he erupted, and suddenly he was looking more tight-lipped than ever. 'You'll be telling me next,' he said, his voice ominously quiet, 'that he's never so much as talked of marriage to you!'

What could she say? Heartily wishing that she had never clapped eyes on Sloan Illingworth, or Toby Keston either for that matter, Whitney regretted that she had ever picked up that wretched phone to dial Sloan's number.

'He has, hasn't he?' Sloan kept up his aggressive questioning. 'He's proposed to you! And you—you replied . . . ?'

'I replied, no!' Whitney flared and, despite having never before felt remotely like hitting anyone, she felt sorely like lashing out at Sloan just then. It went against everything that was sensitive in her to reveal to a living soul the unrequited feelings of another, and yet she just had!

She particularly wanted to strike Sloan, though, when, with her admission that Toby had proposed and had been turned down still in the air between them, he went on to sneer, 'And you have the gall to tell me that you and he are "just good friends"?'

Not liking his tone one little bit, Whitney almost hurled something hot and strong back at him. She stayed silent, though when she realised that, on the face of it, it looked as if she was an out-and-out liar, and she guessed that

that had just earned her several black marks in Sloan's book. Especially when she had the feeling that, apart from this instance when for the sake of his mother's health he was prepared to deceive his parent for a short while, he otherwise had no time for lies.

Trying to ignore the fact that he had been such a bear all evening, Whitney made a concentrated attempt to eat some of her main course. Her concentration had slipped a little, though, when, in the process of dissecting a mushroom, she suddenly discovered that she was venturing into analysing why Sloan was in such a brutish mood. Could it be that his business in Switzerland had not gone well? Whitney discounted that theory. Apart from the fact that, somehow, she just could not see Sloan failing in anything he set out to do, she saw him as a man who would take a business disappointment on the chin, so that few other than himself would know about it.

His mother, then? Whitney rooted some more. It went without saying that he cared very much for his stricken parent. Was she worse than he was perhaps conveying? Whitney scrapped that theory too, and munched with every appearance of enjoyment at her side salad. If Mrs Illingworth's health had badly deteriorated, then it was for sure that Sloan would not now be dining with a woman whom he had *no* feelings for, but would far more likely be at his mother's bedside.

Certain, then, that Mrs Illingworth had not suffered a relapse, Whitney felt her heart suddenly give one almighty bump. For, out of nowhere, but probably triggered by the thought that Sloan had no feeling for her, the idea was suddenly conversely in her head that the reason why he was acting as if every one of his toe-nails was ingrowing was that he was—jealous! On a reflex action her head jerked up—and quickly down. Her own eyes had come into direct contact with the cold, grey steel in his, and it was not jealousy which she read there, but utter dislike.

Rejecting the crazy notion that Sloan could in any way be jealous that she was seeing another man on some of the nights when she didn't see him, Whitney asserted herself enough to know that she could not be more pleased about that. She definitely didn't want Sloan to be jealous, she thought decidedly. Though, of course, that he should be was definitely a crazy notion, because he was still in love with Gleda Caufield.

Having chased her thoughts around, Whitney was feeling very much at odds with the world when, coming full circle, she realised why Sloan was being such a cantankerous devil that evening. Wearily she came to the obvious conclusion that Sloan, not normally one to hide behind lies and deceit himself, hated that trait in others. Plainly, it was sticking in his craw that he thought he had found her out in a lie over Toby.

'Sloan...' she said, and had raised her eyes to his again when a sudden shriek of laughter from a woman who had just entered the restaurant with a man attracted Whitney's eyes in their direction, and she halted.

She was never quite sure afterwards what she had been going to say to Sloan, although it was most likely something along the lines of trying to convince him that she had been telling the truth when she had told him that she and Toby were only good friends. At any rate, she rather thought she had been about to try to convince Sloan that she had not lied to him. But when she recognised the woman who had just come in, every thought went out of her head.

Suddenly, although she had little to feel guilty about, Whitney felt the warm colour of guilt flush her cheeks. For as she recognised the female as a woman who worked at Hobson's Garden Implements, her old firm, her eyes lighted on the man who escorted her, and Whitney saw that her escort was none other than Dermot Selby!

'What ...!' Sloan began, his shrewd eyes noting her change of colour and the way her eyes had strayed from him to somewhere to his left. But Whitney was hot, confused, and suddenly she felt quite sick inside. Unaware that Sloan's eyes had followed hers to where the over-loud couple were waiting for the head waiter to come and show them to their table, Whitney knew only that she needed some air.

'Can—we—go?' she said jerkily to Sloan, and she was in too much of panic then to consider the niceties of waiting until they had ordered dessert.

Dragging her gaze back to her own escort, she observed in his unsmiling, all-assessing look that he had taken everything in and had missed little. But, just as more panic smote her that it looked as though he was going to insist on staying to finish his meal, suddenly Sloan was getting to his feet.

'I've had about enough, anyhow,' he muttered, and she guessed then that he hadn't been enjoying the evening any more than she had.

Leaving his seat, he came around to her, and she felt his hand clamp possessively on her elbow. She was glad of his tall, manly strength as they moved towards where Dermot, without bothering to lower his voice, was half turned to the woman he was with and to whom he was exclaiming that, although the restaurant was expensive, only the best was good enough for her.

Wincing, Whitney's stomach turned over as she recalled how she had been thrilled when Dermot had said something very similar to her. If there had been a back way out she would have used it. But suddenly Dermot and his extra-marital activity were bang in front of them, and were blocking their progress.

'Do you mind?' Sloan's cold, cultured tones suddenly cut across Dermot's amorous glances. 'My fiancée and I would like to pass.'

Immediately, Dermot stepped to one side but, as he did so, he caught sight of Whitney and, clearly forgetting the way they had parted, just as he clearly forgot that he was with someone else, he exclaimed, 'Whitney!' and sounded every bit as though he was overjoyed to see her.

Whitney had no chance to decide whether or not she would have answered him, or what she would have said. For abruptly Sloan was pushing her onwards, and Dermot, who was quite tall himself, was overshadowed by Sloan, and Whitney's vision of her ex-man-friend was lost.

'Go and wait in the car,' Sloan instructed, and as he handed her his car keys, so all at once Whitney lost a little of her inner turmoil, and realised that of course one simply did not just walk out of a restaurant without paying.

Only when she was sitting in Sloan's car as she waited while he settled the bill did she blanch at her gauche behaviour. Suddenly she was feeling weak with embarrassment at what she had done, and, as she gave a despairing groan, she wished for the umpteenth time that evening that she had never rung Sloan and told him, 'So, get your sails hoisted—I'll be ready at eight'.

Though, as she remembered the way he had told Dermot, 'My fiancée and I would like to pass', she felt a shade warmer towards Sloan than she had all evening. There had been no need whatsoever for him to refer to her as his fiancée, and yet, perhaps because he had perceived that her pride could do with some support, fiancée was what he had called her.

Her gratitude to him, not only for the 'fiancée' remark, was total. For, without asking questions, Sloan, after a flicked glance at her, had wasted no time in getting her out of the restaurant. When she saw him making his way towards his car, Whitney was ready to forgive him anything. The fact that he had been impossible for most of the evening was as nought to her as she prepared to give a smile and to thank him for his one hundred per cent support just now.

Her smile never made it, nor did her 'thank you' get uttered. One look at his grim expression when, without a word, he got into the car and set it in motion, was sufficient to tell her that nothing had changed. He might well have complied without protest to her request that they go, but, remembering his comment of 'I've had about enough', Whitney realised he was still being impossible—and cold with it.

Whitney's pride woke up to give her a nudge, and she was certain then that she couldn't have cared less if he never said another word. Her warmer feelings towards him were very definitely in cold storage when, with not one syllable having passed between them, they reached her flat.

The way things were going, it would not have startled her in the slightest had Sloan forgone his usual courtesy of going up to the front door with her and unlocking it. Indeed, anticipating that he would wait no longer than for her to vacate his car and then speed off, Whitney did not wait for him to come round to the passenger's side. As soon as the car had stopped, she quickly opened the door and got out.

Surprise number one came in that before she could wish him a cool goodnight, she found that Sloan had left his car and was standing on the pavement beside her. Surprise number two came when, after going up the concrete steps with her, he took her key from her. When he had unlocked the door and handed the key back, the cool goodnight she was about to bring out of its reserve still never got uttered. For as her chin tilted a fraction and she began, 'G...', so Sloan, with a determined sort of glint in his eyes, interrupted her.

'It's early still, and about time I saw the inside of your flat,' he told her crisply, and, having eliminated any chance that she might think of the excuse that it was too late to invite him in, he made great cracks in her conscience when he told her, 'You can make me the after-dinner coffee I didn't get before I start my drive back to Heathlands.'

There were many things Whitney would have liked to do, but to make Sloan a cup of coffee was not one of them just then. Just then, she would by far have preferred to go to her bed and bury her head under her pillow in the hope that the morning would not find her cringing with embarrassment at the memory of her panicky actions in that restaurant. But Sloan had a fair drive in front of him and if he was parched for a cup of coffee...

'Come up,' she invited, and was conscious of him beside her every step of the way. 'Come in,' she said at the door of her flat, and did not know why she felt unable to have even a stilted conversation with him. There had been times when she had gone out with him when they had just talked and talked, but this was not one of them. 'Take a seat,' she told him as pleasantly as she could now that the role of hostess had suddenly been thrust upon her. 'Black or white?' she queried, knowing that he did not take sugar, and observing that he was more interested in the pictures on the walls of her tidy sitting-room than in 'taking a seat'.

'Black,' he replied evenly, taking his eyes from a watercolour which she had liked and had saved up for.

Whitney dived into the kitchen and suddenly realised that she felt rather shaky. Was it her imagination, or was Sloan tense about something? Telling herself that she was being idiotic, she deftly made two cups of coffee and tried to settle her inner disquiet that, although she could never remember feeling ill at ease with Sloan before, she now felt decidedly discomfited.

Sloan was still on his feet when, with the coffee on a tray in her hands, she joined him in the sitting-room. She had thought that she had got used to his height, but she was suddenly very much aware of him towering over her as he came and took the tray from her.

Hurriedly Whitney pulled out a small table and placed it between two easy chairs. 'If you'd like to put it down here,' she said politely.

She felt better able to breathe when, having placed the tray down on the table, Sloan waited only until she was seated and then took the chair opposite her. However, although she had been grateful to him that he had acted on her plea to leave the restaurant, without asking questions, she was soon made to realise that his non-questioning compliance had been out of consideration for the moment only. Sloan, she was to learn, was the type who insisted on knowing the ins and outs of every-thing!

For she had done no more than handed him his cup of coffee when he was asking bluntly, 'What was all that about?'

'All what?' she attempted, but one look at the hostile expression that came over his features was enough to tell her that she should have known better.

'If there's nothing else between us, at least let there be honesty!' he rapped icily, and while Whitney was conceding that, aside from the dishonesty they would practise in the good cause of his mother's return to full health, Sloan was otherwise the soul of honesty, he had barked curtly, 'That loud-mouth back at the restaurant was ready to fall on your neck before you snubbed him!'

Loud-mouth! Snubbed him! Whitney was trying to cope with the fact that Sloan considered Dermot a loud-mouth when she realised that, since she could not for the life of her remember saying a word to Dermot when he had exclaimed her name, yes, she must have snubbed him!

'Are you trying to tell me that you'd never met the man?' Sloan snarled, when in fact she had not only told him nothing, she had not even answered him. Perhaps that was why Sloan was growing so irate. He was used to people jumping to do his bidding, and answering questions when he put them. 'You'll be telling me next that you wanted to leave that restaurant for no other reason than that you suddenly took a dislike to the décor!'

Whitney's only dislike at that moment was for one over-large brute who went by the name of Sloan Illingworth. 'You know it was nothing of that sort!' she found her voice to tell him shortly. 'I just... It was just...'

Her voice petered out. Her emotions were private, and she was hating him intensely that, having backed her into a corner, he did not appear likely to stop until she told him everything there was to know. *'Damn you!'* she suddenly exploded, when all at once his waiting, watching silence got to her. 'You know all about Dermot Selby; I told you about him, I know I did!'

'He's the man who hurt you,' Sloan stated. His voice had gone quiet, but tough-sounding, and as Whitney had suspected, he had instant recall. 'Why leave?' he charged then. 'Why not stay and face him? Ah,' he said before she could say anything, 'you were afraid that he might hurt you again?' His expression darkened and, with his chin jutting at an aggressive angle, Sloan suddenly fired, 'Does that mean you still think you love him?'

But by then Whitney had no idea what her over-whelming impulse to leave the restaurant on seeing Dermot had all been about. By then she could not even remember when, if ever, she had told Sloan she loved Dermot. And for that matter she felt too confused just then to know whether she did in fact still love Dermot. But what she was not confused about, and what she was very sure of, was that she had had more than enough of Sloan Illingworth!

Whitney blatantly ignored the way he had acted quickly to get her out of that restaurant when she had been ready to panic, and instead she chose to remember the complete swine he had been for the main part of the evening. Mock fiancée or no, surely there was only so much which she could be expected to put up with?

She got up from her chair, and in freezing tones she hinted, 'If you've finished your coffee...'

That glint she wasn't too happy about was again in his eyes when, taking his time, Sloan uncurled his long length. Whitney felt a shade shaky as he stood over her and she became aware that he was much too close for comfort. But, considering that any step which she might take away from him might be construed as a sign of weakness, she determined to stand her ground.

'Thank you,' she began, like the well-brought-up person she was, but when it came to adding anything to that, she was suddenly sunk. She could hardly thank him for a pleasant evening, could she? The words would stick in her throat. 'Drive safely.' She dropped out the platitude and then looked up—and very nearly panicked again.

The smouldering look she saw in Sloan's eyes made her catch her breath. He wasn't impressed by her 'Thank you', and he certainly hadn't liked her platitude, and if she was not mistaken she was his least favourite person just then. Despite his look, which warned that she might do well to take cover, Whitney stubbornly persisted in not moving an inch. She was more shocked than shaken, though, when suddenly his hands snaked out and he caught hold of her in a vice-like grip.

'You've been asking for this all evening,' he gritted beneath his breath, and while all at once she was transfixed and, imagining all sorts of assault, could not have moved then had she wanted to, unexpectedly his head came nearer and the only assault she received was his punishing kiss to her lips.

For an astounded second, Whitney remained motionless. But in the next second, anger and fury were roaring to life, and she was reacting like a wild thing.

'Don't you . . .' she gasped as she pulled her head back and broke his kiss. It was all she had time for. Suddenly one of his hands was clamped on the back of her head, and while that hand held her steady, the next she knew was that, with his other arm around her, Sloan was hauling her close up against his body, and his mouth was once more over hers.

Desperately Whitney tried to break away from him. To try to kick his shins, though, was, she discovered, a dangerous pastime, because it only resulted in making her off balance, which subsequently resulted in Sloan's hold on her tightening more firmly.

Resorting to pummelling and punching wherever she could, Whitney found, however, that with her arms somehow anchored by Sloan, she made little progress in her efforts to get free in that direction either.

He was still continuing to kiss her while Whitney, trying to think up some ploy that would secure her release, suddenly found that she was going haywire. For she should have been plotting and planning how to make Sloan break his hold, but all at once his kisses were gentling and, oddly, all her brain was telling her was that she did not want to break free and that she was, in fact, more than happy to be in his arms!

When his lips did finally leave hers, Whitney was quiet in his arms. Had she been able to speak earlier, she would have called him 'swine' along with a few other names, but, as she looked up into grey eyes which no longer seemed to be cold, all she could think to say was a bewildered, 'Sloan!'

If in that one word, his name, she had given him a message, then Whitney was mindless to what that message was—until, gently, he trailed kisses from the corner of her slightly parted lips and down the side of her throat.

Then, 'Oh, Sloan,' she cried, and she knew, in that moment, that she wanted to stay in his arms and never leave them.

At the sound of his name once more on her lips, his mouth returned to hers, and as the pressure of his lips increased, Whitney pressed her body against him, wanting to get closer, and closer still.

She heard the groan that escaped him as their two bodies seemed to meld as one in a tremendous heat of yearning. Whitney was in a no man's land of wanting when his hands came either side of her and he pulled the lower half of her body yet more strongly against his firm body.

'Oh, Sloan!' she cried breathlessly, and as he kissed her again she knew that, as she was aware of his need for her, so he was aware of her need for him.

Nor could she deny it. She wanted him. She wanted him to make love to her. She almost told him so, but— something disturbed her. Some sound. But only as the sound came a second time did it penetrate as being that of Erica's familiar tattoo.

Whitney's heart was beating like an express train when she realised that the sound of someone at the door had got through to Sloan, too. But, as she stepped back and his arms fell to his sides, she was far, far from remembering what had happened to make him take her in his arms in the first place.

Which was perhaps why her shock was such that it left her speechless when, after the way they had just been with each other, Sloan should tell her in an ice-cold voice, 'Take it from me, sweetheart, if you can turn on like that for other men, then you sure as hell aren't in love with any loud-mouth by the name of Selby!'

Utterly stunned, all Whitney was capable of doing was standing there and numbly watching while he crossed to her flat door and opened it. She was still too paralysed to move when she heard Erica burst into speech with, 'Oh, I'm sorry, I didn't know Whitney had company.'

Whitney was making rapid strides to get herself together when she heard him reply, with a pleasantness that hadn't had an airing all evening, 'I was just leaving.'

Swine, Whitney berated Sloan yet again as she went to the door and saw his departing back as he went down the stairs. 'Come in, Erica!' she cried gaily, hoping he would hear. She then had to work very hard to make it appear as though she had not for one moment forgotten that Erica had said she would pop back later to borrow a hat.

Swine, Whitney hadn't finished berating Sloan when she eventually lay down in her bed that night. There had been no need for him to tell her she was not in love with Dermot Selby, no need at all. How could she be in love with Dermot, when she had known, from the moment she had faced the fact that she was more than happy to be in Sloan's arms, that the only man she was in love with was him—Sloan Illingworth?

CHAPTER SEVEN

WHITNEY opened her eyes on Sunday morning, and quickly closed them. But the knowledge, the staggering knowledge which had woken with her would not be shut out as easily as the daylight. She opened her eyes again and faced the fact that she was in love with Sloan Illingworth.

Stepping out of bed, she prepared to get on with her day, aware now of the wealth of difference between the love she had felt for Dermot Selby, and this all-consuming emotion which being 'in love' had created in her. With Dermot, she had retained some measure of control; with Sloan, there had been no control, nor had she wished there to be.

She made herself a cup of coffee, reflecting on her lack of self-control when she had been in Sloan's arms last night and had wanted him so much. Before, she mused, as she stared into space, she had always managed to retain some awareness of what she was doing. Last night, she had been unthinkingly willing to go wherever Sloan led.

Recalling that the closest she had ever come to going to bed with a man had been with Dermot, Whitney no longer wondered what it was that had prevented her from making that final act of commitment with him. She had not been 'in love' with Dermot.

That morning, Whitney supposed that she should be grateful for Erica's timely interruption. Sloan had desired her, Whitney knew that, but had not exuberant

Erica come beating out the first few bars of *The Teddy Bears' Picnic* on her woodwork, Whitney had no idea what would have happened.

Pride, of course, had her wanting to believe she would not have let him make complete love to her. But Whitney was more honest than that, and she knew that, her resistance gone, she would not have backed away from making that final commitment—with Sloan.

Which was fairly galling when, not much later, she recalled the way he had left her flat without a goodnight. 'Take it from me, sweetheart,' he had said, 'if you can turn on like that for other men, then you sure as hell aren't in love with any loud-mouth by the name of Selby.'

She was on her fourth cup of coffee of the day when she at last squarely accepted the fact that, although Sloan might have desired her, the only reason he had begun to kiss her was to prove that she did not love Dermot Selby. Whitney knew then that she was going to make fully certain that Sloan never discovered who it was she did love.

She put a bright face on when she went into work on Monday, but she had to admit that, with Sloan so much in her mind, it was no wonder to her that she had forgotten all about Toby Keston until, at five to one, he appeared in her office doorway.

'You've forgotten!' he accused when she looked up in some surprise to see him waiting there.

'No, I haven't!' she denied firmly, but she was forced to do a lightning playback of the last time she had spoken with him before she could add, 'Er—just let me finish this,' she indicated the work in her typewriter, 'and I'll be ready to take you to lunch.'

Toby was as sweet as he had always been over that lunch, Whitney reflected when she went home that night. As eager as ever to please, he had put a brave smile on when he asked her out and she told him she couldn't see him at all that week.

'Even Saturday?' he had queried, just the same.

Particularly Saturday, Whitney thought on remembering Sloan's cutting remarks over the phone last Saturday when she had told him she already had an engagement for that evening. 'I'm afraid so,' she told Toby.

But when she waited all Monday evening for a phone call from Sloan, and then all Tuesday and all Wednesday evening too, and not once did her phone ring, she began to realise that she might not hear from him again.

I might just as well have told Toby I'd go out with him, she thought unhappily on Thursday evening, setting the kettle to boil to make a warm drink before going to bed, because her phone had stayed silent all that evening too.

Her pride took a battering when the awful thought struck her that the reason why Sloan was not going to ring again was because of her eager response to his kisses! Quite clearly he had no wish for an emotional liaison of any kind with her and must, equally clearly, have thought up some alternative for his mother's benefit.

Recalling, though, how his mother's return to full health had been his prime concern, through everything, Whitney could not help wondering at that last thought. By the time her kettle had boiled, however, her pride had recovered and she knew, unquestionably, that should he ring—and she realised that there was every chance he would not—then she would tell him quietly but firmly that, though she was truly sorry about his mother, she did not want the role of his fiancée any more.

Having decided, most assuredly, on her campaign of action—just in case he did ring—Whitney was more than ready to welcome company when Erica knocked on her door.

'One hat,' she said on being invited in, 'and one piece of christening cake. Which,' she added, 'since I'm starving, I thought we could share with whatever sort of drink you're making.'

Having not eaten very much herself that day, Whitney felt she could do justice to the cake. And it was over cake and cocoa that Erica told her the details of the christening and how her hat had been much admired.

That topic done with, she just had to rush on, 'I've been bursting a gasket to try and get all my jobs cleared up so I could come and see you, but this has been my first chance. Tell me,' she begged, 'just tell me that I didn't break anything up between you and that dishy-looking bloke when I came hammering on your door last Saturday night. I just couldn't live with myself if...'

'As Sloan told you,' Whitney quickly cut in, 'he was about to leave when you...'

'So *that's* Sloan Illingworth!' Erica exclaimed. 'I'd have asked that night about him,' she went on thoughtfully, 'only, well, you seemed to be in a quiet sort of mood once the front door had closed, and I felt I was a bit of an intrusion, and ...'

'Dope!' Whitney scoffed. 'If I was quiet on Saturday it was because...' Somehow, without meaning to, Whitney found that in order to try and make Erica feel better, she was telling her about Dermot Selby and his latest coming into the same restaurant where she and Sloan were dining.

'Oh, love,' cried Erica in instant sympathy. 'It will soon stop hurting, I'm sure.'

And although Whitney now felt more angry over Dermot Selby than hurt, she had to accept Erica's sympathy. For she found that she just could not discuss with her the real cause for her quiet mood—her discovery that she was in love with Sloan. Because, like the passion that had flared between them, her love for Sloan was essentially private.

Whitney was sleepless in her bed that night. A hundred and one things went through her mind, though with Sloan always the central theme, and she suddenly found that she was wondering why seeing Dermot Selby in that restaurant had made her panic the way she had.

It did not take her long to find the answer. She must have been teetering on the brink of discovering that she was in love with Sloan even then. Seeing the man whom she thought held her heart while she had been out with the man who really and truly *did* hold her heart must have brought about a confusion of senses which had manifested itself in panic. Dermot had wilfully deceived her and, aware as she now was that he was married and had children, was it any wonder that she should feel besmirched that she had ever gone out with him? But for opportunity and her subconscious knowing that it was not true love she felt for him, she might well have gone to bed with him! Was it any wonder that nausea had risen up in her and had brought about the overwhelming feeling of wanting to leave the restaurant?

Whitney eventually fell asleep knowing that whatever Sloan was, or was not, he would never deceive her. She awoke at first light, knowing that she was never going to see him again, so she had better stop thinking about him.

That being easier said than done, she spent most of that Friday trying to eject him from her mind. But, although her telephone stayed silent again that evening, he was in her head again when she went to bed that night.

It was just after ten the following morning, when Whitney was in the middle of cleaning her kitchen floor, that the phone, which had stayed silent all week, suddenly bleeped for attention. Knowing that she would be on a fool's errand if she rushed to answer it, she rinsed her hands and dried them before going into the sitting-room. As though hypnotised, she stared at the calling instrument, then, on shaky legs, she went over and picked it up.

She opened her mouth to say hello, but all at once her throat was so dry that no sound would come. Just as she was thinking that her caller might be having the same trouble, suddenly, and to set her heart pounding, she heard Sloan drawl, 'And there was I thinking you'd gone out!'

Gripping the phone hard, Whitney had to swallow before she could speak. 'I was in the middle of washing the kitchen floor,' she told him fairly evenly, and sent her eyes heavenward that, when he must be used to the most sophisticated conversation, she could, without trying, trot out the dreariest titbits. 'Actually, though,' she said, desperately searching for some follow-on conversation piece, 'I'm going out shortly.' Oh, grief, she inwardly groaned, and knew that love, the fact that the man she was in love with was on the other end of the phone, was responsible for the fact that her brain seemed to have seized up and that, to her ears, she was sounding more moronic by the second.

'I see,' Sloan said, his drawl gone as he enquired levelly, 'Are you going out for the whole day, or will you be free this evening?'

Her heart did an energetic cartwheel. She remembered how last Saturday Sloan had arrogantly assumed that she would be free to go out with him. But, could *she* assume that he was *asking* her out this Saturday?

'Oh, I'm only popping out for a few bits of shopping,' she told him, and she felt her heart make another energetic upsurge when he said,

'I'd like you to spend the evening at Heathlands—can you make it?'

Heathlands! He wanted her to go to Heathlands! Straight away Whitney realised that Mrs Illingworth must have come out of hospital and must be at Heathlands recuperating. There was not a thought in her head then of how, should Sloan ring, she would tell him quietly but firmly that she did not want to play the role of his fiancée any more. In fact, she was no longer thinking of his mother either when she replied, 'Er—how do I get there?'

If her hearing wasn't wildly inaccurate, she thought Sloan sounded much relieved when he replied, 'I'll call for you, naturally. Shall we say six o'clock?' Her heart did another merry dance at his words.

It took Whitney some time to settle down after Sloan's phone call. She finished her chores and took herself off shopping, but her spirits were soaring. Only then did she realise how bereft she had been all that week with no communication from him.

She was back in her flat when she appreciated quite why Sloan had not been in touch with her all that week. And suddenly her relief that he had not been put off by her enthusiastic response to his lovemaking was absolute. Not that anything like that was going to happen again. But plainly the reason why he had not been in touch was because he must have been busy in making the arrangements to have his mother transferred from the hospital to his home.

Mrs Illingworth must have been somewhere close by too, when he had been making that call, Whitney comprehended. That would account for him not saying too much on the phone. But, by saying he would like her to spend the evening at Heathlands, when she had never so much as set foot in his home again since the night of that party, he had conveyed just the same the message that she was to meet his mother.

Overjoyed at the thought of seeing Sloan again, and of spending a few hours in his company, Whitney found even the fact that she was going to pretend to be his fiancée in front of his mother undaunting. She loved him, she was in love with him, and though she would guard with all she had against Sloan seeing that love, Whitney realised that if she did slip up in any way, then she had the perfect cover in that, for his mother's sake, she was merely acting the part.

It crossed her mind to consider taking Mrs Illingworth some flowers. It was a natural enough thing for a future daughter-in-law to do, she thought. Against that, though—what if Mrs Illingworth did not like flowers, or worse, thought her pushy?

Whitney rejected the idea of taking flowers, and she was ready by five-thirty and was in the throes of an attack of the jitters. At a quarter to six she thought she had her jitters under control, but when, five minutes later, her flat bell went, she sprang from her chair as though on a piece of elastic.

A hasty look out of the window showed that it was Sloan, or at least that was his car parked by the kerb, which confirmed that it was he with his finger on the doorbell. Whitney took one last check of her trim shape in full-skirted primrose and white two-piece and, snatching up her brown shoulder-bag, she left her flat.

She felt a wave of warm colour rush to her face as she opened the front door and saw Sloan standing there. She desperately needed to find something bright and witty to say to hide the fact that she was remembering his ardent kisses and that just to be with him again was joy to her, but the best she could come up with was, 'What's the traffic like?'

'About usual for a Saturday,' Sloan replied, eyeing the picture she made in her primrose and white with some admiration. 'Fit?' he asked, and at her nod he took hold of her elbow and piloted her down the steps and into his car.

Her whole body still felt alive from his touch when Sloan turned on the ignition and headed his car in the direction of Heathlands. Nervous of giving her feelings away with some careless remark, when throughout the drive Sloan seemed disinclined to talk, Whitney decided to stay silent herself. With his mother waiting for them at Heathlands, Sloan no doubt had a lot on his mind. Whitney gave herself up to the pure pleasure of just being with him.

She could not deny a few panicky moments when he pulled up at Heathlands, however. Too late, she realised that she should have spent all these weeks leading up to this moment finding out what must be dozens of things she should know about Sloan and didn't.

The house seemed quiet when he unlocked the front door and stood back for her to precede him inside. 'You remember where the drawing-room is,' he said, and she was not sure if he said that because his mother might be in earshot, or to remind her that she had been in his home once before, and that now she must be prepared to pay for the disastrous outcome of that one visit.

'Yes, of course,' she replied, and, for once, she did not rebel at his blackmailing reminder. He had his reasons for doing what he was doing and she—she was in love with him, and did not want this time with him to stop.

Fully anticipating that Mrs Illingworth would be in the drawing-room, Whitney felt full of tension as she walked into it. But there was no one there!

'Your—mother?' she queried, half turning to look at Sloan.

He seemed to hesitate, she thought, but Whitney soon realised that that was because he wasn't quite sure what her question meant. 'She's—well,' he said, after some moments of deciding that she must be asking after his mother's health. 'Now,' he went quickly on, 'can I get you something to drink?'

'Er—nothing for the moment,' Whitney declined, and as Sloan indicated that she should take her ease in one of the comfortable-looking, well-padded chairs, she went and sat down. She was about to make some comment of pleasure that Mrs Illingworth was maintaining her progress to full health after her journey to Heathlands, but what she had been about to say somehow got lost when Sloan asked to be excused for a minute or two.

'We'll have dinner in about half an hour,' he went on. 'But before we can do that I must first obey Mrs Orton's instructions and go and turn the oven on.'

True to his word, he was away for only a brief while. In that brief while though, Whitney had had time to realise that the housekeeper must be doubling up as nursing aide as well. She must, Whitney thought, at this very moment be either getting Sloan's mother ready to have her dinner in bed, or helping her to dress so that she could come downstairs for a short time.

Only when Sloan returned to the drawing-room did Whitney discover how wrong she had been. 'Everything turned on?' she asked him lightly when he came back and occupied one of the chairs nearby.

'Everything,' he replied, and as he looked at her, a trace of a smile came to his expression as if he liked what he saw.

Whitney liked the look he wore. She liked his smile; it did funny things to her insides. And all at once, with her eyes still on his mouth, the mouth that had kissed hers, she became aware that her heart was thundering. She was certain he could not hear it, but her love for him had thrown her so much that she found she had broken into hurried speech, saying the first thing that came into her head.

'I was unsure whether or not to bring flowers,' she told him.

For a second or two Sloan looked at her blankly. Then suddenly that trace of a smile had turned into the grin which, she realised now, had been the start of her falling in love with him. 'There's no need,' he told her, and there was a teasing look in his eyes. 'Mrs Orton cooked the dinner; I merely turned the oven on.'

Sloan's grin had flushed out her own. That he should tease her so merrily was a pure delight to her. 'Not for you,' she scorned with a light laugh. 'I thought about bringing flowers for your mother, only...' Something in Sloan's look as his grin fell away told her that she had got it wrong somewhere.

'You thought that my mother was here?' he asked, his face suddenly deadly serious.

Whitney nodded, and then, as it came to her that Mrs Illingworth wasn't there, she wondered if something dreadful had happened to her. She then remembered that Sloan had said his mother was well, and in any case he certainly wouldn't have been grinning his head off at her as he had a moment ago if his parent had taken a turn for the worse.

'Oh,' she said softly, and she revealed her thoughts to him when she told him, 'I thought, with you inviting me here as you did, that your mother was out of hospital. I thought,' she went on quickly, hoping that Sloan didn't think her too much of a fool, 'when you said you had to turn the oven on, that Mrs Orton was upstairs helping your mother.'

'The only person Mrs Orton is helping at the moment is her daughter,' Sloan told her. 'At present my housekeeper is having a lovely time babysitting for her daughter who lives in the next village.'

'Oh,' Whitney said again, and realised that she had jumped to far too many conclusions. She took it more slowly this time when, more feeling her way than assuming, she questioned, 'So before she went, Mrs Orton cooked dinner and . . .'

'And left everything ready for us. All I had to do, I was informed, was to set the oven at the right temperature half an hour or so before we wanted to eat.'

Whitney opened her mouth and very nearly said 'Oh' again. Quickly, she closed it. For while she was sure that Mrs Orton had never told Sloan anything so vague as to turn the oven on for half an hour 'or so', the words 'left everything ready *for us*' had sounded beautiful in her ears.

'Perhaps I'd better—er—go and have a look in the kitchen?' she suggested.

When Sloan's grin came out again, Whitney knew that she was absolutely besotted with him. And when, with charm that melted her backbone, he replied, 'I was hoping you'd say that,' there was nothing she would not do for him.

The kitchen, as she remembered, was the largest kitchen she had ever been in, but Whitney, with her thoughts in a whirl, was hard put to it to keep her attention on the casserole which was warming up nicely in its cast-iron pot.

Had Sloan invited her to Heathlands because Mrs Illingworth *had* been coming out of hospital, only her departure from hospital had been cancelled at the last minute? Whitney discarded that theory when she recalled that it was only that morning that Sloan had telephoned her and had asked her to spend the evening at Heathlands. He'd have known by then about any change in his mother's plans. It must all be connected with his parent somehow, though, she decided. Most likely, with her discharge from the hospital due any day now, Sloan wanted to be able to let drop a remark in his mother's hearing to the effect that they had recently dined together at his home.

'It's coming along beautifully,' she told Sloan as she turned away from the eye-level built-in oven, and at the friendly look he gave her, she did not care what reason he had for inviting her to Heathlands. She was there, with the man who held her heart, and, as she recalled how Sloan had once remarked to her at an art gallery 'And I rather think I like you', she thought that he *had* grown to like her, and she was happy.

Having decided to enjoy her evening with him, Whitney had no room in her head for asking herself questions which, on her form so far, would only bring her wrong conclusions anyway.

Whether the shaking off of the responsibility of asking the whys and the wherefores of everything had any bearing on how much more agreeable she found that dinner with Sloan, Whitney could not have said. Maybe it was just that, having accepted the fact that she was in love with him, there was a new awareness in her where he was concerned. But, whatever was responsible, as they ate their way through their cold starter, and then ploughed into the casserole, Whitney knew that she had never been happier in her whole life.

The meal had been punctuated by an easy flow of conversation, with Sloan listening as if he was really interested in anything she had to say. When he was not listening he was entertaining her with an anecdote or two which had made her laugh.

They were tucking into warmed-through apple pie and cream when Whitney glanced up and saw that he had paused in his eating and was watching her from across the table. She smiled at him simply because she felt like smiling. She saw his eyes go down to her mouth and then, as his eyes returned to hers, she saw a slow, gentle smile begin on his mouth.

Her heart did another of its giddy somersaults, and she looked at her pudding plate; concentrating on her pie, she saw from beneath her lashes that Sloan too had recommenced eating.

'More?' he asked when he observed her placing her spoon on her empty plate.

'Not another crumb!' she refused lightly.

'Coffee in the drawing-room, then,' he decreed, and when she said that she would make the coffee, Sloan wouldn't hear of it. 'Away to the drawing-room, woman,' he told her sternly, the upward lift at the corners of his mouth denying his severity. 'You weren't supposed to do a thing this evening, yet you've supervised everything that's come out of that oven.'

'You exaggerate,' Whitney told him cheerfully, and, because it seemed that he wouldn't have it any other way, she went off happily to the drawing-room.

She was joined by a tray-carrying Sloan some ten minutes later. 'Never spilt a drop,' he boasted, and Whitney loved him still more.

The evening had gone from mere enjoyment to being enchantment-filled as far as she was concerned when, after handing her a cup of coffee, Sloan went and put on some background music. In companionable silence they sat near to each other and drank coffee while music wafted softly through the room. Earlier, one of Sloan's anecdotes had made her feel near to tears from laughter. But now, with Sloan unspeaking and seeming to her as though he too was finding enchantment in the evening, Whitney felt that tears were near because everything was so, so beautiful. She never wanted it to end.

But it had to end. She had long since finished her coffee when, with a start of amazement, she caught sight of her watch and she saw that it was half-past ten. Staggered at the way the time had raced, she dragged her eyes from her watch to feel concerned that before Sloan could get to his bed that night, he had to drive her to London and make the return trip to his home.

'Washing-up,' she said, apropos of nothing.

'Washing-up?' he exclaimed, not with her at all, which didn't surprise her, since she guessed that he probably couldn't remember the last time he had had his hands in washing-up water.

'I've got to think about getting home,' she told him, and explained, 'I just can't leave someone else's kitchen the disaster area we've made of Mrs Orton's.'

Sloan hesitated, and seemed as though he was just about to forbid her to wash so much as a teaspoon. Then all at once he relented. 'We'll do it together,' he said, but qualified gravely, only the smile in his eyes as he looked at Whitney giving away that he wasn't serious, 'Though I'm sure Mrs Orton would enjoy clearing it up when she comes back tomorrow.'

'I'm sure she would,' Whitney laughed, and while she carried the coffee tray with the used cups and saucers into the kitchen, Sloan went to the dining-room to retrieve any remaining dirty dishes from there.

As she had once before, Whitney decided not to use the dishwasher lest she turned the wrong dials. Sloan had about as much idea as her how to set it in motion, but Whitney soon had a sink full of hot suds. Never had she ever thought that there was anything even remotely magical about washing dishes, but as one piece of china after another was rinsed off, magical was what she felt it to be.

All because of Sloan being there to dry each piece, she knew that as she half turned to hand him the last of the china before she lifted the cast-iron casserole dish off the side to set to work on it. He had turned from her to place the plate in his hands on the table of clean dishes at the back of her when Whitney stretched out a soapy hand to the casserole dish. She was in a dream world where Sloan was in truth her fiancée, and her attention was anywhere but on what she was doing when his voice, sounding strangely strained and for all the world as if he was nervous, suddenly startled her.

'Whitney,' he began, 'I've got to t...' What he was going to say, though, was unexpectedly cut short by her cry of alarm as the cast-iron dish she had just picked up started to slip from her sudsy fingers.

Even while she was rejecting the impression she'd had that Sloan had sounded in any way nervous, for goodness' sake, Whitney was making valiant efforts to catch a firm hold of the falling casserole. But, all in the split second of Sloan startling her and breaking off from what he was saying at her cry of alarm, the dish had escaped her fingers and, hitting the water heavily, caused Whitney to be in receipt of the splash-back.

'Ugh!' she cried, as warm, sudsy water penetrated the front of her top right through to her skin. Because of her inner happiness, though, a light laugh left her as she turned, looking for a towel.

'You're soaked!' Sloan exclaimed, coming forward with a towel and unthinkingly stretching out a hand to where her primrose and white top was plastered wetly to her breasts. Changing his mind, he handed the towel to her and made the instant decision, 'That's going to take for ever to dry. Come with me, I'll get you a dry shirt.'

'There's no need,' she tried to protest, mopping at herself while conceding that he was right and that the top half of her two-piece was going to take an age to dry, but more concerned with what a clown she was going to look in his over-large shirt when she only ever wanted to look her best for him.

But, as though Sloan was aware of every one of her thoughts, he growled, 'You'd look good in anything, and you know it, so stop being stubborn.'

'Well, if you put it like that...' Whitney murmured, but he was already leading her by the hand from the kitchen.

They were both smiling when they went upstairs, he perhaps from amusement at her humorous way of giving in, and Whitney simply because she loved the whole feeling of togetherness with him.

At the door of the room which she knew to be his bedroom, Sloan let go of her hand and opened the door and went in. Her eyes followed him when he went over to his chest of drawers, but she could not stop her gaze from going over to the huge double bed while he opened one of the drawers and extracted a shirt for her.

Her thoughts strayed back to consider that if she had never wandered into this room that night of the party, she would never have met Sloan.

'Don't stand there,' he said warmly as he turned to see that she was still standing in the doorway. 'You can change in here. I'll...'

He broke off as Whitney, ready to obey his smallest command, came forward, her expression dreamily gentle. 'This is where it all began,' she said softly, but instantly she wanted the words back, because she just did not want to remind him of his broken engagement or of Gleda Caufield, the woman he had loved, and must still love.

But, to her utmost joy, she discovered that she had no need to withdraw the words because, quite unbelievably, as she halted in the middle of the carpet, Sloan came and stopped in front of her, and she distinctly heard him reply, 'And I, for one, can't say that I'm sorry.'

Seconds ticked by as, looking up into grey eyes that seemed to hold a warm light for her, Whitney realised that what he was saying was that he wasn't sorry that he was no longer engaged to Gleda. 'Oh, Sloan,' she gasped as it dawned on her that his words must also mean that he was no longer in love with his ex-fiancée, either!

'My—dear,' he breathed, and as if it was pre-ordained, meant to happen, and as if nothing could ever prevent it from happening, he dropped the shirt he had been about to hand her on to the foot of the bed, and the next moment he had gathered her tenderly into his arms.

Almost reverently then, Sloan kissed her. And, his hold gentle, he pulled her closer to him. And it was all so beautiful for Whitney that tears welled to the surface. Sloan, Sloan, my dear, dear Sloan, she wanted to whisper for him to hear as her hands reached up to touch his face.

He broke his kiss, and turned his head to kiss her palm, and there was such a tenderness about him that again she wanted to cry out his name.

But she did not cry out his name. What she did say, though, when he turned to look down into her upturned face, was a choked-sounding, 'Your shirt-front will be as wet as my top if...'

'Have you heard me complaining?' he teased softly.

Whitney shook her head, and soon she had forgotten about her soaked top, and the fact that Sloan's shirt was getting damp too. Because he was kissing her again, and one kiss did not seem to be enough.

Her arms were wound tightly about him when she felt his hands come beneath her top. His touch was warm, and was seeking, searching as his hands caressed to her midriff, and then caressed to the back of her.

She felt his hands at the fastening of her bra, and even though she had made no demur so far and had given him every encouragement, or so she thought, she could only love him more when, before he undid the fastenings of her bra, he softly enquired, 'All right with you, Whitney?'

Too full to speak, she nodded, and she knew her reply had been received when, her fastenings undone, she felt his hands at the naked skin at her back. When that same warm, gentle touch caressed round to her front and he held each swollen globe of her breasts in his hands, Whitney knew that she had consented to anything he asked of her.

'Oh, Sloan!' she cried in delight and anguish of wanting when his fingers tormented the hardened peaks he had created.

'I want you, sweet Whitney,' Sloan breathed. 'Is it the same with you?'

'You know it is,' she said huskily, and gave him her lips, feeling only the first pangs of shyness when he went to remove her top. 'C-can we have the light out?' she asked, and it seemed that, even if Sloan was not aware of the reason for her request, he was ready to grant her anything. Because, leaving her for only a moment, he plunged the room into darkness.

When he came back to her, he was without his shirt, and Whitney gloried in the freedom he allowed her as her hands roved over his broad shoulders and she caressed her way round to the front of his chest.

Then, with the minimum amount of fuss, 'Put your arms up, sweet love,' Sloan instructed her, and in a few seconds her top had been disposed of, her bra along with it, and Sloan's hair-roughened chest was against her silken skin.

Again she wanted to cry his name, and might well have done, but suddenly his lips were claiming hers, and his kiss was deepening, and Whitney knew then, as her need for him soared to match his desire for her, that there would be no turning back.

In the darkness they stood together, and in that darkness Sloan undid her skirt. Whitney stepped out of it when it slid to the ground, and she clutched on to Sloan as he removed the rest of her clothes.

Almost carried by him as, caressing her, kissing her, he moved to the bed and divested himself of his clothing, Whitney knew only that she was in love with Sloan and that this was right for her.

'Sweet Whitney,' he breathed, and, as his mouth came over hers, he moved with her on to the bed and pulled down the covers.

In an enchanted world, she knew nothing but the delight of the touch of the man she loved as he trailed kisses down her throat to finally capture her breasts. 'Sloan!' she cried as his fingers did magical things to her spine. And, 'Sloan!' she cried again when her need was more than she could bear.

She was ready to beg him to take her when he at last moved his body to her. But her cry of pleasure was suddenly diminished at the first shaft of pain. This time she did not have to call his name or say anything. For Sloan immediately knew what her cry of pain had been about. What her shy wish to have the light out was all about. She knew it the instant his body stilled.

'Oh, my G...!' he exclaimed in an awed kind of voice. 'Oh, my dear—you're a virgin!'

But Whitney, her desire for him greater than her pain, was suddenly in dreadful fear that Sloan might not want her.

'Please,' she implored him. 'You can't leave me like this. I want you, I need you.' Ready to beg, she clung to him.

'Oh, my love,' Sloan cried, and as Whitney gripped him and held him close to her naked body in panic that he might go from her, 'Oh, my very dear Whitney,' he breathed hoarsely, and gently, his touch so considerate that it was almost ethereal, he tenderly made her his.

CHAPTER EIGHT

Dawn had tiptoed through the night sky when Whitney stirred in her sleep. On any other Sunday, she might have turned over and slumbered on, but for some reason she felt compelled, this Sunday morning, to open her eyes.

Pink colour washed her creamy cheeks as her waking green eyes fastened on the bare masculine chest which was only inches away from her gaze. A warm, dreamy smile picked up the corners of her mouth, and her eyes travelled upwards until she met, full on, the grey eyes of the man who was propped up on one elbow and who had been observing her while she slept.

She did not feel shocked to see him there; only, as memory raced in of how they had lain naked with each other and were still naked, a little shy.

But her shyness appeared to delight Sloan, for as she looked at him, a tender smile appeared on his mouth and in his eyes. 'Hello, my love,' he whispered, and it was then that Whitney, with an overflowing heart, knew that Sloan loved her.

'Hello,' she whispered back huskily, and she began to tingle anew when, beneath the covers, his arm came around her waist and he pulled her naked body towards him and kissed her.

With his mouth gently teasing her lips apart with tender kisses, Whitney was soon more glorying in their nakedness with each other than overwhelmingly conscious of it.

'Oh, Sloan,' she cried shakily, and she knew more rapture as his hands caressed her body and he brought her to the peak of desire.

'Am I allowed to look at you now?' he asked tenderly, reminding her of the way she had wanted the light out last night.

Unable to tell him yes or no, Whitney's answer was in the way she gave him her lips in utter supplication. Gently, unhurriedly, Sloan uncovered her, and gently he kissed her belly, her breasts, and her mouth.

'You're more than beautiful,' he told her, and as he kissed her again, and as their bodies touched, he looked tenderly into her eyes and promised, 'Sweet love, it will be better for you this time.'

It was still early when Whitney awoke for the second time that morning, but when she opened her eyes there was no Sloan propped up on one elbow looking down at her. Nor was his head on the pillow beside her.

Then she heard a sound somewhere in the house, and she realised that perhaps the sound of Sloan moving around downstairs was what had awakened her a few moments ago.

For some minutes she lay there just glorying in the way she and Sloan had been with each other. Never had she imagined that she would know such total freedom with him. To touch him, his body, as he touched her.

Whitney supposed that she should be feeling a little shocked that, when she'd had no plans to spend the night away from her flat, she should not only do that, but should spend the night in bed with Sloan. But, loving him with all her being, she did not feel shocked. More, she felt warmed through and through and sublimely elated, for the simple reason that as she loved Sloan, so Sloan loved her.

Of course, he hadn't said that he loved her. Not in so many words he hadn't. But, as Whitney left the bed to go to the adjoining bathroom to turn on the shower, she knew that love her he did. She had only to remember the way they had made love at dawn to know that. For the way he had made love to her that second time was, in contrast to the first, as thrilling as it was staggering.

Only then had she realised how, for her untutored sake, he had kept a rein on his passion the first time. His thought then had been more for her than for his own needs, she was sure of it. Which had to mean that he loved her, didn't it?

Realising that doubts were starting to edge in about something over which she had been pretty near certain only a short while ago, Whitney showered hurriedly. She needed to see Sloan again. She needed to have that re-assurance that it was as she believed, that he did love her.

Feeling that she would only have to see his face to have the truth of her thoughts endorsed, Whitney quickly dried, and she was soon dressed, save for the primrose and white top which had come to grief while she had been washing up last night. She had the top in her grip when, on the floor by the foot of the bed, she espied the shirt which Sloan had been about to hand her when he had instead gathered her into his arms.

She wasn't even thinking when she dropped the garment in her hands down on to the bed, and got into Sloan's over-large shirt instead. Rolling up the sleeves as she went, she left the bedroom in some haste, wanting to see him, and went swiftly down the stairs.

As she reached the hall, a sound in the drawing-room attracted her attention and, as a stray trace of shyness suddenly made itself felt, she slowed her pace. But, as she approached the drawing-room, she saw that the door was open, and her need to see Sloan suddenly became greater than her shyness. She had stepped inside the room when she stopped stone-dead. For the person there was not Sloan but, busy with a duster, his housekeeper. And Whitney, who had never in her life before left any man's bed to be confronted by a housekeeper, did not know how to handle it. Especially when the look on the housekeeper's face made it plain that, though it wouldn't take her long to guess that she had shared her master's bed, she had not until just then so much as known that she was in the house.

'Good morning, Mrs Orton,' she tried to cheerfully brazen it out.

'Good morning,' Mrs Orton mumbled in reply, but she had nothing else to add, and Whitney felt more uncomfortable than ever. Suddenly she was overpowered by the knowledge that she had on Sloan's shirt, and any ability she had to brazen the situation out promptly deserted her.

Wishing that Sloan, with his easy sophistication, would come and extract her from this uncomfortable moment, Whitney, growing a shade more uncertain that Sloan did in fact love her, found that she was looking for excuses for why she had stayed overnight.

'I—er—expected Mrs Illingworth to be here,' she volunteered. And when the housekeeper looked at her blankly, and gave every impression of seeming not to have the first idea of why she should have expected her employer's mother to be at Heathlands, Whitney suddenly caught on. 'Oh, it's all right, Mrs Orton,' she smiled. 'I know all about Mrs Illingworth being—a little—confused.'

'Confused?' Mrs Orton repeated, and while Whitney was thinking what a loyal person she was, the housekeeper went on to give Whitney her first inkling that something was wrong. 'If you're referring to Mr Illingworth's mother, she's Mrs Eastwood now,' she stated, and while Whitney was taking in the news that Sloan's mother had remarried at some time, she was adding, 'But I don't know where you got the idea from that she's confused, I'm sure I don't. I spoke to her myself when she telephoned Mr Illingworth yesterday, and although we didn't talk for very long before I went to find him for her, she was as bright and alert as she ever was.'

'Oh—I see,' Whitney said slowly, trying to get over her surprise at what the housekeeper had just said by being glad that, by the sound of it, Sloan's mother was making rapid strides back to full health. 'Well, I'm glad that Mrs Illing... Mrs Eastwood,' she corrected herself, 'is so much better after her accident. I...'

'Mrs Eastwood hasn't been in any accident!' Mrs Orton informed her, and seemed astonished that Whitney should think she had.

Shaken rigid, Whitney refused to listen to what her intelligence was trying to tell her. 'But when she phoned yesterday, she must have rung you from the hospital,' she insisted brightly.

'Hospital?' Mrs Orton exclaimed, astounded. But Whitney was the more astounded of the two, though utterly stunned was a more accurate description of how she felt when the housekeeper told her, 'Mr Illingworth's mother didn't ring from any hospital, she rang from her home in America.'

'America!' Whitney echoed stupidly, one part of her brain just refusing to function and accept what the housekeeper was telling her.

'Mrs Eastwood's husband is an American, so they decided to live there,' Mrs Orton said, as if that explained everything.

As some receptive part of Whitney's brain began to acknowledge that Sloan must have lied, lied, and lied to her, her heart started to fracture. By some great good fortune, though, her plentiful supply of pride began to stir. And as she started to hurt with a pain such as she had never known, Whitney was aware that only she was going to know it. Even as Mrs Orton stood there, having answered her questions only because, clearly, she wanted to get on and tidy up the drawing-room but was too polite to dust while her employer's guest was addressing her, Whitney was biting down the pain.

Spotting her brown shoulder-bag down by the couch, she masked her hurt by going over and bending down to pick it up. 'I must have got it wrong about Mrs Eastwood's accident,' she said over her shoulder.

'Must have,' Mrs Orton agreed, and went on as Whitney delayed in straightening up, 'I've only become acquainted with her in the year I've worked for Mr Illingworth, but I've never heard of Mrs Eastwood having a day's illness—and,' she added as Whitney straightened, 'she wouldn't have phoned to say that she and her husband had made up their minds on the spur of the moment to take a cruise, and would be away two months, if there was anything the matter with either of them.'

'She certainly wouldn't,' Whitney agreed, but she was aware that, though outwardly calm and composed, she was breaking up inside. Pride alone was responsible for the smile she showed the housekeeper as she told her, 'I must be on my way.' But, along with pride, rage was starting to nip, and latent murderous traits were beginning to make themselves felt. 'Do you know where Sloan is?' she asked pleasantly.

'The doors of the particular garage he uses were open and his car was gone when my son-in-law dropped me off on his way fishing,' Mrs Orton replied.

'Oh, he's probably out somewhere, then,' Whitney said, only by pure grit managing to keep her smile in place as it hit her that, by his very cavalier attitude, Sloan was making it seem as though she was nothing more than—than a—one-night stand! Appalled that that was about all she was to him, Whitney's rage was momentarily buried and she knew only that she had to get out of there, and fast. 'It was nice meeting you again,' she murmured, though as she went from the room Whitney doubted that the housekeeper would remember her from their previous meeting. She hoped, with all she had, that she would forget this meeting too.

Whitney was in the hall and was about to leave Heathlands when, at the solid front door, her swamped feelings began to revive. She was already starting to feel angry again, when, in the act of hitching her shoulder-bag further over her shoulder and simultaneously stretching out a hand to the door, she became aware that she was still wearing Sloan's shirt.

And suddenly, she was infuriated. As she recalled how she had lovingly wrapped the shirt around her when she had put it on, Whitney's rage went into overdrive and was almost past enduring.

Without any memory of how she had climbed the stairs and came to be on the first-floor landing, Whitney went storming into Sloan's bedroom, her shaking fingers already tearing at the buttons of the shirt. It was impossible for her to keep her eyes averted from the over-large bed, and she hurled Sloan's shirt from her.

Sparks were shooting from her eyes as she claimed her primrose and white top and, without regard to its damp and creased condition, put it on.

Out of the love she bore him, she had given herself to that—that rat. But to him she was just a one-night stand! Her outraged gaze went to the pillows where their two heads had lain, and suddenly it was past enduring.

In a flash Whitney had her bag open and her lipstick in her hand. Without needing to think what she would write, in the next instant she was over at the head of the bed.

A minute later, she stood back to admire her handiwork. Good, she thought, and hoped the 'I'll never forgive you, *ever*' which she had splashed in lipstick over his pillow would never wash out.

Whitney had only a faint recollection of how she got back home to her flat that day. She had some vague recall of having run the first half-mile, and then of having hitched a lift with a lorry driver. But what the lorry driver had looked like, or what, if anything, they had spoken of, she had no idea. All she could think of, and the thing which dominated her thoughts that day, was how everything was a lie.

She had thought that what she had shared with Sloan had been shared in mutual love, but it had not been. She had thought there had been no need to speak of love because the way they had given of themselves to each other had been a declaration of love, but she had been wrong. It had all been a lie. All of it.

Whitney went to work on Monday still trying to come to terms with what a credulous fool she had been. No wonder Sloan had never asked her to go with him to visit his mother in hospital—his mother hadn't jolly well been in any hospital! She hadn't even been in England, but was where he had known perfectly well she was all along: at her home in America!

'Yes?' she snapped when Toby Keston had the misfortune to stop by her office that morning.

'Oh, I'm sorry,' he apologised, and despite having done nothing to apologise for, he looked so downcast that Whitney laid the sin of her snappy temper at Sloan Illingworth's door as well. 'Is it something I've said?' Toby asked.

'No,' Whitney relented to assure him quickly. 'And it's I who should apologise, not you. Now,' she spared him a few minutes from her day, 'what can I do for you?'

'I was wondering, actually, if you'd like to go out somewhere tonight? We could...'

'I'm sorry, Toby,' Whitney stopped him right there. 'I'm—just not very good company at the moment. Do you mind if we leave it for another time?'

'You're not ill, are you?' he fussed, when Whitney just wanted to be by herself.

'No, I'm not ill,' she told him, bringing all her reserves of patience to bear in view of her earlier impatience with him. 'It's just that—I have a few things I need to work through at present.'

With that, Toby had to be satisfied. But when Whitney went home that night, her thoughts went on the same old treadmill, and she went to bed with her bitterness against Sloan not one iota minimised. How could he have acted the way he had?

Memories of Sloan haunted her on and off through the night. She had thought Dermot a rat for taking her out while he had a wife at home, but she thought that the lies which Sloan had told her made him the bigger rat of the two.

She hated deceit, and had only squared her conscience about the deceit she would have practised on Sloan's mother by knowing that it was all in the good cause of his parent's return to full health. But when Whitney thought of how Dermot had deceived her, and of how

Sloan had deceived her, what she hated most of all was men!

And he'd actually had the nerve to say to her one time, 'If there's nothing else between us, at least let there be honesty.'! Whitney's head was still teeming with thoughts of Sloan when she left her flat to go to her office on Tuesday morning.

She made her way home having faced the fact that she had been deliberately set up. The answer which had eluded her for the last two and a half days came as she put her key in the front door. As Whitney turned her key in the lock, she realised why Sloan had acted the way that he had. At first she couldn't believe that he had done what he had out of his need for revenge because, but for her, he would still be engaged to Gleda Caufield. But, far-fetched though it seemed, nothing else would fit but that, his love lost to him, he'd set about making Whitney fall in love with him so that she too would know how it felt when the loving stopped.

Oh, he'd done it very subtly. Because it wasn't until as recently as ten days ago that he had kissed her and she had realised that she was in love with him. He too, she now saw, must have realised how she felt about him.

Inside her flat, she cringed inwardly as she acknowledged how gullible she had been, for Sloan had deliberately left it a week before he had got in touch with her again. A long, long week had passed, and he must have known that she would have rushed to do anything he asked her when he eventually telephoned.

And what had he asked? Not that she go to bed with him; he was too subtle for that. He'd used the opportunity of his housekeeper's having the night off to his own advantage, though, hadn't he? Not that he could have foreseen that she would get herself half drenched the way she had when they had been doing the washing up, but Whitney did not doubt that Sloan would have got her to his bedroom one way or another.

She sighed a shaky sigh as she remembered the way she had reminded him that his bedroom was where it had all started. 'And I, for one, can't say that I'm sorry,' he'd replied, and she had thought that he was not in love with Gleda any more.

Which, Whitney realised, he might or might not be, but it was certain that he was not in love with Whitney Lawford either. Stirring up her hate against Sloan when thoughts of him and his bedroom brought forth a flood of memories of the unexpected tenderness she had received from him, Whitney was ready to deny ten thousand times that Sloan had for an instant held back on his own need in order to reduce her pain to a minimum.

He was a swine, a rat, and she doubted if he ever had any intention of bringing her back to her flat that night. From the start, she now plainly saw, Sloan had intended that she should spend that Saturday night at Heathlands, in bed, with him. Well, if the 'I'll never forgive you, *ever*' which she had splashed in lipstick all over her pillow had not knocked on the head any idea he might have that she was in love with him, then she only hoped that the fates would be kind to her, and would give her another chance to get that message across.

The fates were with her, she was to discover before she went to bed that night, although at first she did not fully appreciate the fact. Sloan was still in her head, as she was beginning to realise he was going to be for some time, when someone came tapping on her door. She went to answer it, knowing that since it was not Erica's knock, and since the outside door was always locked, her caller had to be someone who lived in the building.

'Hello, Joseph,' she greeted the beaky, bespectacled fifty-year-old school-teacher from the ground-floor flat.

'Whitney, dear lady,' he beamed. 'Sorry I didn't come up before, but I've been having an argument with my spin-dryer.' So saying, he handed her a large but fairly flat-looking parcel. 'Arrived special delivery, as I came home tonight,' he intoned. 'Hope it's not too important.'

'I'm sure it isn't,' she replied, having not been expecting a parcel, and finding even a special delivery parcel something over which she could not drum up any enthusiasm. 'Who won?' she asked. 'You or the spin-dryer?'

'The contest isn't over yet,' he told her, and spent a few more minutes in idle chat before he added, 'Well, I'd better return to things domestic, though I seem to have far fewer screws and washers than I started out with.'

Whitney went back inside her flat and studied the clearly printed address label without receiving a glimmer of enlightenment. Realising that there was only one way in which she was going to find out what the parcel contained and who had sent it, she went and fetched a pair of scissors and set about getting rid of the outer covering.

Three minutes later, she was rocked to her very foundations. For, enlightened, she felt tears sting her eyes so that she had to blink them back before she could take another look at the navy-, orange- and red-bedaubed canvas which she knew full well was entitled 'Mirth', and which she had, in Sloan's company, once admired.

She had no need to read the signature on the piece of notepaper which had fluttered down to the floor. But, as she bent to pick it up, her heart, denying that she hated Sloan, started to thud out an uproarious clamour as she owned to wanting to know what he had written.

It did not take her very long to read what Sloan had penned, though as her heartbeats started to steady down, it took her longer to know what to make of his 'I bought this some time ago—I thought you might like it'. But when she did know, she was angry, and was hating him again.

Her first thought was to write a neat little note saying, 'You thought wrong!' and to return the canvas to him. But the more she thought about it, the angrier she grew. How could he? she fumed. How dared he? she raged. Just *who* did he think he was?

Whitney realised that Sloan, by concocting the story about his mother's illness in his endeavour to have revenge on the woman who was responsible for his engagement coming to grief, had shown himself to be an eye-for-an-eye man. She had never been more offended in her life, for what had also just now become clear was that he was a man who would be beholden to no one.

He had left her with little choice but to go out with him. But every move he had made thereafter had been calculated to ultimately get her to fall in love with him, when he would take her to his bed. And, by doing a disappearing act when she went to find him the next morning, he would thereby have rejected her. What he had not calculated on, though—and Whitney knew that there had been nothing pretended about his shock—was his discovery that she was a virgin.

Picking up the scissors, Whitney looked at the painting which she had once thought lovely, and, needing only to remember Sloan's last lie, 'I bought this some time ago', when it could only have been yesterday at the earliest, she summoned up the fire and furious energy needed to slash it from corner to corner. And, finding she still had energy to spare, she slashed the canvas from corner to corner in the other direction. The picture, she knew, had worn the price tag of five hundred pounds, but, as she stood back to survey her handiwork, she would not have cared had it cost twenty times that amount. So Sloan Illingworth would be beholden to no one, and thought to salve his conscience by sending her the consolation prize of a five-hundred-pound painting, did he? Well, let him hang this on his conscience; she jolly well hoped it weighed heavily.

Whitney was late in getting to her desk the following morning. More important than being at her office on time was the urgent parcel which she had had to stop off with and send by special delivery.

Days passed, but there was still pain in her heart when in the late evening, two weeks to the day since Sloan had taken her to Heathlands, Whitney sat in her flat and wondered when, if ever, she was going to start to get him out of her mind and heart. She hadn't heard another word from him since she had returned that painting. Not that she had expected to hear from him. In any case, she promised herself stoutly, she would give him very short shrift should he so much as *dare* to phone.

Certain what her reaction would be should Sloan try to get in touch with her, Whitney could do nothing about the way her glance went to the phone as if imploring it to ring.

Grief! As though she cared, her pride assured her loftily, but she was glad when she heard Erica's footsteps coming down the stairs, followed by her tattoo on her door. Whitney felt she could do with some company other than her own.

'I've decided that all work and no play makes Erica a dull girl,' Erica grinned as Whitney invited her in. 'There has to be time for me, don't you think?' she asked as she followed Whitney into the kitchen and watched while she put the kettle on.

'It depends what you want from life, I suppose,' Whitney replied, sensing that Erica was feeling serious behind that grin.

'I suppose so,' she agreed, and confessed, 'I thought I knew what I wanted, and then—I met Chris.'

'Ah!' murmured Whitney.

'Ah, indeed,' Erica sighed. The cocoa had been made and they were seated in Whitney's sitting-room when Erica went into the depths of how isolated she felt on the nights she told Chris that she couldn't see him because she was studying.

'Er—how does he feel—on the nights you say you can't see him?' Whitney asked.

'That's just it! I don't know, and I wish I did. He's a sweetie really,' Erica went on, 'so I shouldn't complain, but if I say that I'd like to do this, that or the other, he says all right, and seems to enjoy the places we go together, but... Oh, I don't know,' she said glumly.

'Perhaps you're working too hard,' Whitney suggested. 'Perhaps you need a rest, or perhaps need to take time out to get a long-distance view of things.'

'You could be right,' Erica agreed and putting a smile on her face, she asked more cheerfully, 'How's *your* love-life? I don't see signs of Toby tonight.'

'I saw him last night,' Whitney told her, and did not have to say any more.

'Getting too regular, is he?' Erica cottoned on, adding, 'If you feel like that, kiddo, then he obviously isn't the one for you. Oh, by the way,' she said suddenly, 'there was a picture in the paper today of that industrialist who you went out with a couple of times.'

Whitney had been out with Sloan a good many more times that just a couple, though, since she had not been so open about him as she was about her other dates, Erica was not to know that. Well aware, however, who

Erica was speaking of, aside from Sloan being the only industrialist she knew, she allowed several seconds to go by before querying, 'Oh, you mean Sloan Illingworth?' And then, because she just could not hold the question back, though she did manage to make her voice sound only just as interested as it should, she added, 'What's he been up to? I didn't get a paper today.'

It was gone midnight when Whitney, after rinsing the cocoa mugs which she and Erica had used, climbed into bed to lie awake and think about Sloan. So much for any nonsensical thought that he might phone to take her to task about that picture or even—should she be so crass as to imagine he would—call in person to tell her that one did not go around doing things like that to works of art. Although, from memory, Sloan hadn't been at all impressed by that particular painting.

Shrugging aside the weakening thought that in that case he had only bought it because she had liked it, Whitney did not for a minute regret her action. She hoped his conscience crippled him. Though, from what Erica had said, Sloan had been photographed at an airport on his way to the Far East, and had looked 'dead dishy', so it didn't seem as though he was having any trouble with his conscience. Apparently Sloan, according to the paper, had no idea when he would be returning to England.

Another week went by, during which Whitney faced the fact that though she might have told herself that she hated Sloan, hate him she could not. But she knew better now than to think that she might answer her doorbell one day to find him standing there—the last time he had journeyed in an easterly direction, he had been out of England for three months!

Four weeks to the day since she had last seen him, Whitney sat herself down and took herself to task. She couldn't go on like this, not eating, not sleeping properly. Sloan Illingworth had deliberately deceived her, had lied to her—about his own mother!—used her, and had thrown her aside. He was just not worth her losing so much as another wink of sleep over.

Having given herself something of a very severe talking-to, over many hours, Whitney went to work on Monday morning determined that should Sloan Illingworth stray into her head then, by the quickest route possible, she was going to push him straight out again.

Events, however, were fast catching up with her. Feeling more cheerful than she had of late, she greeted Toby brightly as she came upon him in a corridor. She never got to hear his reply, for just then, without warning, everywhere started to spin and, as she tried to cry out, everything went black.

She came round from her faint to find that Toby, looking worried to death, had one arm around her and a hand to her head, while a couple of other people were locked in a debate about whether it would be better to push her head down between her knees, or if she should have her feet propped up on something.

'I'm—all right, now,' she croaked to whoever wanted to hear, feeling more embarrassed than ill.

'I'll take you home,' Toby peered into her face to offer.

'I don't need to go home,' Whitney told him. 'I'm quite all right,' she said, keeping to herself the fact that, as she tried to get up, her legs did feel a little wobbly.

Grateful that Toby still had his arm about her, she then had a verbal tussle with him when she wanted to go forward to her office, and he wanted to turn her about and head her to the car park.

'If you won't let me take you home, then at least let me take you to the works' nurse,' he pleaded.

'Oh, Toby,' Whitney cried peevishly, embarrassed still, and starting to feel a fraud as she began to realise that her faint just now was no more than her body protesting at her lack of interest in food just recently.

She was in the middle of silently vowing to push some breakfast down tomorrow morning if it killed her when the man she worked for came along and Toby, catching Mr Parsons' glance at the arm he still had around her, explained, 'Whitney just fainted,' and that did it.

All this fuss, she thought irritably when, in her embarrassment, she walked away from both men. Toby was soon after her, taking hold of her arm and guiding her. But since in truth she didn't have much sense of where she was going, she found that he'd had his way and that he had guided her to the nurse's office.

'Miss Lawford just fainted,' he told the solid-looking, no-nonsense nurse.

'Did she, now?' that lady boomed. 'Well, we won't need you, for a start.'

Poor Toby—Whitney saw that he looked totally taken aback, and after he had gone she had to smile at his expression. She was not smiling, however, fifteen minutes later, when she too left the nurse's office.

Feeling stunned, she went to her own office and, having assured Mr Parsons that she was perfectly well, she sat down at her desk reeling from the import of the questions which were chasing around in her head after her discussion with Nurse Baker. The nurse had lost her brusque manner as the two of them had talked, but her direct questions had led Whitney up an avenue which— probably because her thoughts were elsewhere so often— she had not paused to consider. In any event, it hadn't taken Whitney very long afterwards to realise that it might not be a bad idea if she had a pregnancy test!

At three that afternoon, she made use of Mr Parsons being absent from the office and, having looked up the number of the Pregnancy Testing Service, she picked up the phone and asked the operator for an outside line.

It was a bad week for Whitney. She went home from her office on Friday evening having that day been acquainted with the news that she was, indeed, pregnant!

Desperately did she need someone to talk to that night. But there was no one. No one in whom she could confide, at any rate. At first she did not know whether she was glad or sorry that her lovemaking with Sloan had brought about the result she had just been told it had. As the evening progressed she started to feel slightly hysterical, and almost rushed up to Erica to confide and to ask her how she felt about being godmother for a second time. But then Whitney calmed down and started to get things a little more into perspective.

The discovery had been a shock, she had to admit that, but the very fact that she was thinking in terms of Erica being a godmother brought about the realisation to Whitney that she must want her baby. Otherwise, surely, she would not even be thinking in that direction at all, but would be thinking in the direction of having an abortion.

As soon as the word abortion entered her head, Whitney abruptly ousted it. She had felt such an overwhelming rush of distaste that she knew that she would protect that new life within her with all she had.

That established, she began to feel better than she had all week. She took herself off to bed early and had the best night's sleep she'd had in an age. At breakfast time, with Sloan again the main preoccupation of her thoughts, she decided that she did not want any breakfast, but her protective feelings rose to the fore once more. She was carrying Sloan's child, and for the child's sake she would have to embark on a healthy diet and see to it that no more meals were missed.

Whitney pushed down a slice of toast and, as if to make up for past dietary failures, poured herself a whole half-pint of milk. And all the while as she sipped at her milk her thoughts were on Sloan, his baby, and what she should do about him in that respect. Should she tell him?

Without hesitation her innate honesty told her loud and clear that tell him she must. Against that, though, was the argument, would he want to know?

For long minutes she dwelt on that question, but, when she considered how he had lied to her almost from the moment she had met him she was unable to come to any firm conclusion.

Having eventually finished her glass of milk, Whitney was clearing away her breakfast things when she discovered that she was turning her questioning back in on herself. Did she want Sloan to know, she found she was asking, or was it that, hungry for the sound of his voice— and presented with a very good reason to contact him— *her* honesty was getting confused by her need to see or to hear him?

Shaken by her fresh thoughts, Whitney grabbed up her purse and took herself off to the local shops. She was buying an extra milk supply when it dawned on her that, since nothing was going to happen for months and months yet, she had no need to make any snap decision.

She was letting herself back into her flat when she realised that, since it could be that she was still reacting from the shock of what she'd been told yesterday, she must not do anything hasty. Anyway, with Sloan still abroad, and for all she knew likely to be so for a few more months yet, she had time to get over her shock before she decided what to do.

In that, though, she discovered that she was wrong. For she was in her kitchen in the late afternoon, making herself a cup of tea, when her phone rang. Guessing that her caller was Toby, she went to answer the phone, realising that, because of her changed circumstances, she would shortly have to do something about him.

But not just yet, she found out. For the voice that enquired, 'Whitney?' as she held the phone to her ear was not Toby's!

Scarcely able to breathe from the shock of hearing Sloan, Whitney sought desperately for something smart, something intelligent, or anything to say that would hide from him the fact that just to hear him had her in a state of near collapse.

'Speaking,' she managed, which, even if spoken coolly, could hardly be said to be either smart or intelligent, she owned. But when a few short weeks ago she might have given him a tart reply and then slammed the phone down on him, her need to hear his voice had her still gripping the phone to her ear. By then, though, the lies he had told her were far from her mind, and so too was the 'I'll never forgive you, *ever*' which she had splashed across his pillow. For that matter, she wasn't even thinking of the decision she had to make about whether or not to tell him that she was expecting his baby. For the moment she had even forgotten that she was pregnant.

It was temper, pure and simple, which made her remember that fact, however. Because her anger was immediate and furious when, after something of a longish pause, Sloan had the outrageous impudence to reply to her cool answer, by drawling loftily, 'Forgiven me for taking your virginity yet?'

On the instant, the proud anger that should have been there before enfolded her. 'My virginity in exchange for an unwanted pregnancy hardly seems a fair swap!' she blazed, and then did what she should have done a minute before. She fairly crashed the receiver down.

Urgh! That man! Fuming, she was too angry to sit still, and she paced the floor, regretting with every step that she had told him what she had.

Not that it mattered, she seethed, when half an hour had gone by and she was still pacing the floor. She had meant to think about it very deeply before she did anything, but it was all his fault! Trust him to make her lose her temper!

Whitney gradually became more composed when she realised that it made no difference anyway. Judging by his past record, the mere fact that he had made her pregnant wasn't going to cause him any lost sleep.

She subsided into a chair and the time ticked by as, with her thoughts still on Sloan, it came to her that by telling him what she had, she could not have made it more of a certainty that she would never see him again.

It seemed, though, that this was her day for getting things wrong. For just then her doorbell sounded. Toby, she thought, and, seeing no time like the present, she went down the stairs prepared to let him be the next person she told about her condition.

Reaching the door, she unlocked it, and then, turning the handle, she pulled the door open. Whitney then came close to fainting for the second time that week. For her caller was not Toby!

CHAPTER NINE

How she managed to stay on her feet, Whitney could not have said. Gripping hard on to the woodwork of the door, she recovered from the feeling of wanting to faint, and heard Sloan asking urgently, 'Are you all right? You're as white as...'

'I'm entirely well!' she told him frostily, backing away when he took a step forward and seemed as though he would offer the support of his strong arms. Staring coldly at him, with her look as frosty as her tone, she felt relief when, although he made no move to step back out of the hallway, his arms dropped to his sides.

'We have to talk,' he said quietly, and when she made no move whatsoever to invite him up to her flat, he demanded, a shade aggressively, she thought, 'Do you want to talk on the doorstep?'

Without a word, she turned and led the way up to her flat. Inwardly she was still all over the place from seeing him so unexpectedly, but the fact that he was there at all showed her that, having received the news that she was pregnant, he must—if she had got it right—want to accept some of the responsibility.

When Sloan followed her inside her flat with a purposeful look and firmly closed the door, Whitney quickly found her tongue. 'I thought you were abroad,' she said in a hostile rush.

'I came back yesterday,' he replied, and asked sharply, 'You've been trying to get in touch with me?'

'Don't flatter yourself!' she bristled, and realised too late that, in the circumstance of her being pregnant with his child, to try and contact him might seem to him to be a natural action on her part. More carefully, though her manner was still hostile, she commented, 'You've obviously been putting in some time at your office since your return.'

'Why do you say that?'

Slightly put off because what was obvious to her clearly wasn't so obvious to him, Whitney was left to explain, 'I just assumed that for you to have got here in the space of time since your phone call meant that you'd rung from your office. Not that it's important where you rang from,' she told him off-handedly, as jealousy nipped that if he hadn't phoned from his office, he must have phoned from a friend's home in London— a female friend?

'As you say, it's not important where I phoned from,' Sloan replied. 'Though in actual fact I rang from Heathlands...'

'You rang from Heathlands!' Whitney exclaimed, startled, realising that he had driven like the wind to get there in so short a time. That—or he was back to his old trick of lying his head off. Sloan was nodding to confirm that he had come straight from Heathlands when the most dreadful thought struck Whitney. So much for her thinking that, if she'd got it right, Sloan had called round because he wanted to accept some of the responsibility! With a sickened sensation she realised that she couldn't have got it more wrong. If he had indeed driven from Heathlands, then the only reason he could have for breaking his neck to get to her must be that he did *not* want to accept any of the responsibility for her pregnancy. That what he wanted was that she should have that pregnancy terminated—with all speed.

Before she could open her mouth to revile him though, Whitney had to hold back when, not deigning to reply verbally to her incredulous 'You rang from Heathlands!', Sloan put the blunt question, 'Is it true?'

She did not pretend to misunderstand him, but the fact that he should dare to question what she had told him nettled her. 'Of the two of us,' she told him waspishly, 'you're the more accomplished liar!'

'Liar!' he exclaimed, just as if butter wouldn't melt.

'My God!' Whitney blazed. 'How you have the nerve to...' Words failed her. 'Yes!' she snapped, 'It's true! I had my pregnancy confirmed yesterday.' She was building up a fine head of steam when she went storming on, 'And if you've broken all records getting here with the intention of telling me to have an abortion, you can...'

'Good God!' Sloan snarled. 'That's the last thing I...' He broke off, and seemed to sense that, with the two of them becoming angrier by the second, nothing was going to be resolved. Though what he was there to resolve, Whitney had less and less idea. Nor was she any further forward when, as he swallowed down his annoyance with her, Sloan looked at her and then said gruffly, 'You look as though you should be sitting down.'

His concern as his hand touched her arm and he moved her to a chair was exasperating to her. But as she sank down into the one chair, while he availed himself of the one opposite, she owned that her legs had felt like jelly ever since she had opened the door to see him standing there—and it had nothing to do with her pregnancy.

'Now,' he said after some moments spent staring at her, during which time she had not said a word, 'let's keep calm, shall we?'

'Very well,' Whitney replied primly, and she managed to stay calm as, just as if he was chairing some business meeting, he outlined,

'The facts, as I see them, are that you're pregnant with my child and, from your tone just now, I gather that you, like me, will not countenance an abortion. Am I right?' he asked evenly.

She was not altogether sure she believed that he did not want her to have an abortion, but in the absence of any proof, and since he appeared to be waiting, a shade tensely, for her answer, 'Yes,' she told him, 'you're right.'

A slow trace of a smile touched the corners of his mouth at her reply, and she stared, fascinated. His smile didn't fully make it, though, and suddenly she had the most uncanny feeling that the man opposite, who must have chaired hundreds of high-powered meetings, was, at this one, feeling as much on shaky ground inside as she felt.

She forgot any such nonsensical notion, however, when, with his eyes steady on hers, Sloan quietly but firmly responded, 'Then, my dear Whitney, the obvious answer must be that you and I—marry.'

'*Marry!*' Utterly astonished, Whitney very nearly catapulted from her chair in her surprise. Had her legs felt strong enough to support her, she probably would have done. But, his suggestion confounding her completely, all she was capable of doing was staring at him in total stupefaction.

Her amazement, however, was to go soaring out of all bounds when Sloan, observing that she had nothing else to say after that one word '*Marry*!', seemed not to have observed that her silence stemmed from nothing more than that she was struck speechless, and he continued, just as if he thought that everything was settled!

'It's Saturday now,' he itemised, when, dumbstruck though she was, Whitney had not forgotten which day of the week it was, 'so I suggest, since we shouldn't delay, that I set the wheels in motion at once for us to be married by special licence. With any luck,' he went sweepingly on, 'we might have the licence through enabling us to be married on Tuesday, when...'

'Now *wait* a minute!' Whitney made a concentrated effort to stop him before he could bulldoze her up the aisle.

'Something wrong?' he queried, for all the world as though he was puzzled by her sharp interruption.

'*Everything's* wrong!' she exploded.

'I'll agree that in an ideal situation it's preferable to marry first and then start a family,' he conceded, 'but since—through no fault of your own——' he inserted handsomely, 'you are—er—in what I believe is termed "an interesting condition" I think we should make every haste to...'

'If it wasn't for my *interesting condition*,' Whitney recovered a little to hurl at him, 'then there would be no question that there just wouldn't be any talk of you and I getting married. As it is,' she rushed straight on when it looked as though Sloan might have tried more bulldozer tactics, 'I have no intention of marrying you, regardless of my *interesting condition*!'

Glaring at him, she observed that it was his turn to appear stunned. Though she discounted the possibility that he was in any way stunned, just as she discounted the impression she had that he appeared to have lost some of his colour too. She was getting to distrust her senses entirely.

'You hate me so much that you'd allow my child to go through life without a father?' Sloan recovered to ask her stonily.

Hate him? Oh, dear God, if only he knew! Fearing that she was weakening, and knowing that she could not afford to weaken, Whitney drew on all her reserves of strength. 'I don't hate you, Sloan,' she told him coldly.

'Maybe I should hate the con-artist you've proved yourself to be, but...'

'Con-artist?' he exclaimed, much in the same way as he'd exclaimed as if he hadn't known what she meant when she had called him a liar. 'When have I ever conned...' He broke off. 'Ah...' he said and halted.

'Penny dropped?' she questioned rudely, and watched as he shook his head, as though to say that this was something he had not reckoned on.

'Somehow,' he said then, 'I don't know how, but somehow, you've found out about my mother, haven't you?'

'And how!' Whitney spat waspishly. 'My stars, it must have been like taking Dolly Mixtures off a two-year-old, the way you took me in to get your revenge.'

'Revenge?' Sloan repeated incredulously. 'What in God's name are you talking about?'

'I don't need this, Sloan, honestly I don't,' Whitney told him, aware of how gullible she had been and still was because, like an idiot, she still wanted to believe every lie he uttered. 'You came to see me as soon as you knew about...' Her voice had faded, but it grew strong again as she resumed, 'Whether you would have gone through with it is a moot point, but you've done the honourable thing and offered to marry me. But now, will you please go?'

She had ended on a shaky breath, and she took her eyes from him to study, without really seeing, the material of the skirt she had on. To her dismay, though, when Sloan moved, it was not to get up and leave, but only so that he could bring his chair nearer to hers.

His chair was half turned and almost touching hers when, from about a foot away, he stated quietly, 'There's far too much between us, Whitney, girl, for me to go— just like that.' Whitney refused to look at him when, still in the same quiet tone, he added, 'I said at the outset that we had to talk—it would seem that I've left my side of the talking a good deal too long.'

'If all you intend to do is to fill me up with more lies, then I'd sooner you didn't,' Whitney told him icily.

'I've finished lying to you,' Sloan told her seriously, and she wanted to believe him.

'Well, you would, wouldn't you?' she said acidly, knowing that she had to deny that gullible streak in her or be lost. 'You've had your revenge from me being the cause of your broken engagement, so...'

'Broken engage...!' Sloan sounded so absolutely amazed that Whitney's head jerked up. She found herself staring into sincere grey eyes as he murmured, 'Oh, my dear, is that what you meant when you spoke before of me having my revenge?'

Whitney swallowed hard on the suddenly dry throat. Sloan calling her 'my dear' was doing nothing for the stiffness she was trying to hang on to. 'I can't think why else you should fill me up with all those lies about your sick mother, when in actual fact your mother is hale and hearty and, far from being in hospital, not even in the country!' she told him shortly.

'She is now—in this country,' Sloan informed her. 'But, God willing, I'll tell you about that later. For now, believe it, nothing I ever said or did where you were concerned was in any way remotely connected with a revenge motive.'

Her heart flipped at the sincerity in his voice. But she'd been fooled before. 'You surprise me!' the person in her who was never going to be gullible again told him tartly.

'At times, I surprised myself,' Sloan confessed, and when Whitney raised her eyes to give him a daggered look at what she saw as an admission of how easy he had found it to lie to her, he asked quietly, 'How long have you known?'

It seemed as if she had carried the weight of knowing around with her for ever, but in actual fact, it wasn't all that long. 'Since my second Sunday morning at Heathlands when I went downstairs and had a—a chat— with your housekeeper.'

'Mrs Orton had returned from her daughter's!' Sloan exclaimed, startling Whitney that though he had instant recall of the occasion, he seemed not to know that his housekeeper had returned to Heathlands! Though, as Whitney remembered how she had woken up to find him gone, she guessed that whatever had made him leave the house before his housekeeper's return could have kept him busy and away from the house all day, so that he would not necessarily know at what time Mrs Orton had returned.

'Her son-in-law brought her back on his way early morning fishing,' Whitney told Sloan sourly. 'How else should I learn, when I mentioned that I'd expected Mrs Illingworth to be there—as I had the previous evening,' she reminded him sourly, 'that your mother's name was not Mrs Illingworth, but Mrs Eastwood? How else,' she asked, 'should I have learned that far from being the confused lady which you had led me to believe she was, your mother had never been in any accident, and had been as bright and alert as ever when she'd phoned from her home in America the day before?'

Whitney had come to a stormy end, and she flicked Sloan an acrimonious look while she waited for him to offer some defence or excuse for the outrageous untruths which he had allowed her to believe. Not that, in her book, there was anything that would excuse those outrageous untruths. But instead of Sloan being the one to flounder, Whitney discovered that she was the one on the defensive when, his expression softening, he murmured, 'Oh, poor love, how vulnerable you must have felt that morning. How it must have hurt you to...' He broke off, and suddenly there was an added alertness in his look as he asked her urgently, 'Was *that* why you wrote that you would never forgive me—because of your discovery of my deception—and not because you thought I'd taken unfair advantage?' Whitney's heart started to labour painfully, but she found herself totally unable to say a word. 'It was the pain my deception inflicted on you and not, as I thought, because I'd unfairly seduced you, giving you no chance to think—when you would have said "No"—which made you leave that message and run from Heathlands. It was...'

But, from being a silent mass of agitation, Whitney's anger had started to spiral. 'Dammit, Sloan!' she cut him off, furious with him that he had gleaned that she had been so hurt that she had 'run' from his home, and furious with herself that her fear of him learning that she had given herself to him from love had made such a coward of her. 'What was I supposed to do when I found out about your deliberate deceit? Was I supposed to stay around waiting for you to come back to exact more revenge?'

'Reven...'

'Yes, revenge!' Whitney stormed. Her temper well and truly alight, she was not prepared to let him get a lying word in edgeways. 'If you didn't know before, then you darn well knew when we—when we...' she faltered before rushing on, 'went to bed together that I'm not the one-night-stand type. How the hell was I supposed to react when, after what Mrs Orton told me, everything fell into place and I realised that you'd treated me as a one-night stand...?'

'My God!' Sloan erupted, looking stricken at the way she had seen events. 'Don't...' But Whitney was beyond giving credence to how he looked and, well and truly wound up, she would not allow him another word.

'How was I supposed to feel to know that you had used me?' she challenged. 'That you...'

'Used you?' Sloan exclaimed, starting to look as angry as she. 'Never!'

'I said *used*, and I meant *used*!' she hurled at him and, her voice rising, she became too angry to remain seated. 'You'd never forgiven me for making use of your bed that night of your homecoming party,' she went rushing on, on her feet and uncaring in her fury that Sloan was standing too and that he was towering over her. 'When your fiancée discovered us sharing the same bed you decided that, since your engagement had been broken in the mistaken belief that you and I had been lovers, you'd have your revenge by making that a fact. You...'

'For God's sake!' Sloan roared, about the only way he could get in to break her flow. 'Why the hell should I want revenge when my engagement to Gleda Caufield was terminated *before* I climbed into bed beside you that night?'

Momentarily stunned, Whitney was too stumped to have anything to come back with. 'Before?' she gasped. But, as plainly as if it had only just happened, she suddenly had a clear picture of Gleda Caufield standing at Sloan's bedroom door and calling her a bitch, adding, 'I hope you're satisfied that, through you, my engagement is over.'

'Huh!' Whitney scorned, and felt an almost irrepressible urge to hit him. '*That*,' she stressed acidly, 'just has to be your biggest lie to date!'

'I'm not lying!' Sloan bellowed. *'I'm...'* Suddenly he checked his anger with her and, seeming to be striving for the calm which he had suggested that they both use, he stretched out a hand and touched her arm. 'We're getting nowhere like this,' he said more quietly. 'Won't you sit down again, Whitney, and—let me explain?'

She favoured him with an uppity look, and she was sure that she had no intention of either regaining her seat or listening to one single lie more from his glib tongue. Though as she stared chillingly into his steady grey eyes she was all at once taken aback that Sloan, being the man he was, was bearing her uppity arrogance remarkably well. All at once, too, she found that she had to wonder why he thought he had to explain anything. If, as she was still certain, the only motive for his actions had been revenge, why, with that revenge taken, would he bother to explain anything at all?

Telling herself that she was more intrigued than interested, Whitney took her eyes from the steady greyness of his and seated herself in the chair from which she had a few minutes before jumped up. As she anticipated that he would, Sloan bent to the chair placed near to hers, though before he sat down he moved it that bit closer, and she realised that, sitting this close, neither could miss a thing in the other's expression. She began to feel a flicker of apprehension.

When Sloan sat down and turned to her, apprehension changed to agitation. Hiding her feelings under a cloak of sarcasm, she remained outwardly uppity to drawl, 'I feel certain that any explanation you wish to make must surely begin "Once Upon A Time".'

She saw from the way his jaw jutted forward an aggressive fraction that her unveiled hint that she believed he was going to tell her only fairy-tales had niggled him.

But she was feeling too shaky inside to feel any small triumph at having scored a minor victory.

'Perhaps I deserved that!' he gritted.

'Only perhaps?' she remained sarcastic to scoff.

'Very well,' Sloan told her stiffly, and, taking a few seconds to consider what he was going to say, he went on, 'In view of my past evasiveness on—certain issues—and, yes,' he agreed, 'a downright lie here and there on occasion, I can hardly expect you to be any other than sceptical.'

'Noble—beyond words!' Whitney tossed in for good sarcastic measure.

'But,' he continued, her sarcasm noted and then ignored, 'I swear to you it's the truth, and that my engagement to Gleda Caufield was broken *before* she confronted you and me in the same bed.'

'Oh, I believe you,' Whitney lied, quite well aware that Sloan knew she was lying, and uncaring of the fact. 'But what a pity that, if you knew you were no longer engaged,' she lost all pretence as hostility entered her voice, 'you forgot to tell your fiancée!'

'I didn't forget to tell her!' Sloan retorted sharply. But, more evenly, he reminded her, 'That party, as you know, was meant as a surprise homecoming organised by my fiancée after my three months away. What you did *not* know, because she had "forgotten" to tell anyone, was that, apprised in a phone call from abroad, expressly advised in a following letter, and verbally informed face to face a few minutes after I arrived at Heathlands that particular night, Gleda Caufield knew that she was no longer engaged to me.'

Whitney could only gasp at his barefaced nerve as he finished speaking, and she lost no time in letting him know how she had received this, his latest basinful of lies.

'You're losing your touch, Sloan,' she told him acidly. 'Your other lies were much more plausible! Though it could have been that, with my own mother suffering confusion after learning of my father's betrayal, and her subsequent death from a road accident, your lies were easy for me to swallow,' she reasoned hostilely, 'but . . .'

'Whitney, oh, my dear!' Sloan uttered softly. 'You told me your mother was dead, but you never said how she had died. I would never have been such an insensitive brute as to use those same circumstances to . . .'

'Well, it's beside the point,' she cut him off shortly as his tone, his sympathy, and the memory of her dear mother all combined to weaken her. 'I'm not likely to believe another thing you say, anyway. As if any woman would go to the trouble to organise a surprise homecoming party for her fiancée when she'd been told, not once, but *twice*,' she scorned, 'that the man she was in love with and engaged to had changed his mind and . . .'

'Gleda Caufield was never in love with me, nor I with her!' Sloan chopped her off, and consequently caused Whitney to stare at him. Dearly would her jealous heart like to believe that he had never been in love with the woman he had been engaged to, but, she realised, that would not alter the facts as they now were, not one iota.

'You'll be telling me next that you were *never* engaged to her!' she flared, as she accepted that even though Sloan had proved himself to be a treacherous rat she could not help but love him still.

'No,' he denied mildly. 'I was engaged to her.' His voice was mild still when he added, 'I was engaged to her and recently overseas when word reached me that she was not being the kind of faithful fiancée she should have been. But only when I realised that I was more annoyed than hurt that she was playing fast and loose while she was wearing my ring did I know that I neither loved the lady, nor wanted to marry her.'

'Oh!' fell from Whitney's lips in a breath of a whisper, when she had not meant to contribute one single sound to this conversation. But she found herself adding more, putting in, 'Perhaps your—informant—got it wrong?'

But Sloan was already shaking his head. 'I checked the information out, and knew I wouldn't be breaking her heart when I put through a telephone call to her,' he replied.

'You rang—to break your engagement?'

'I did,' he confirmed. 'Though as soon as she saw which way the call was going, she pretended that there was something wrong with the line, and that she couldn't hear me properly. But she knew then that our engagement was off.'

'Are you sure she isn't in love with you?' Whitney asked, despite herself.

'Oh, yes,' he said blithely.

He seemed so uncaring of the fact that his ex-fiancée did not love him that Whitney's misbehaving heart gave a happy flutter. She even found herself asking, 'What did you do—after Gleda pretended not to hear you?'

'I hung up, and communicated by mail the fact that the engagement was over.'

'Oh,' said Whitney again, but the days had gone when she believed everything he said without question. 'How come, then, if she was twice acquainted with the fact that she was no longer engaged to you, she organised your homecoming party just as though she was still engaged to you?' she asked. 'Or didn't she say?' she added with a distrustful look.

Sloan bore her distrustful look very well, she thought. He didn't even seem in the least fed up with her questioning, either. In fact, Whitney suddenly had the uncanniest notion that he was prepared to sit there for as long as it took to ensure that not one single question remained in her mind!

'According to her,' he replied levelly, 'she had neither comprehended what I'd said in my telephone call, nor received any letter from me.'

'Perhaps she hadn't,' Whitney suggested.

'It all blew up at the start of my three months away,' Sloan told her, 'and one telephone call and one letter was all she received from me. Innocent as you are, my dear,' he went on—when Whitney was not so certain she could be called innocent any more thanks to him—'I'm sure you're not so naïve as to believe that if Gleda Caufield still thought herself to be engaged to me, she would let another two and half months go by without doing something about it. The least she would have done,' he added, 'would have been to contact my office and ask them to send a telex.'

Whitney clearly recalled the confident blonde, and could not help but agree with him. 'Perhaps—you're—right,' she conceded, and entirely missed the realising that it seemed she was now starting to believe him.

Sloan smiled. 'I am right,' he said softly, and, returning to that fateful night, he said, 'I confess I wasn't in a partying frame of mind when I returned to Heathlands after a three-month, hard-at-it stint abroad.'

'You were—angry?'

'I was tired,' he said, 'and in no mood to find my drive and lawns cluttered up with cars, nor to hear, from the unholy din coming from my house, that I'd got company. All I wanted as I walked in that early morning was my bed.'

'Oh, grief,' Whitney murmured, recalling how she herself had wanted her bed more than she had wanted to be part of the raucous party. 'You—er—soon found Gleda?'

He nodded. 'Very soon,' he told her. 'She must have read from my expression that I was not well pleased, because she asked me in some urgency not to make a fuss.'

'So you just left her to it—and came—er—went to bed.'

Sloan gave her a look that suggested she should have known better, but he told her, 'Fortunately, Mrs Orton had thought to lock some of the rooms. I opened up my study and took Gleda there. It was then that I made short work of telling her, so that she could not be in any possible doubt, that our engagement was at an end, and...'

Whitney guessed that Sloan had been pretty blunt about it, and she could not refrain from butting in, 'Was she upset?'

'Waterworks did seem imminent,' he shrugged, that trace of a smile which Whitney loved hovering about his mouth, 'but she cheered up considerably when I told her that she could keep the engagement ring—which she was still wearing.'

As Sloan must have spotted that Gleda was still wearing his ring, so Whitney remembered that she herself had also spotted the costly-looking sapphire and diamond ring on Gleda's finger—the cost of which must have run into many thousands. 'But,' she had to remind him, 'she definitely still thought she was your fiancée when she stood at that bedroom door. She said...'

'I know quite well what she said,' Sloan interrupted her gently. 'But it was all an act.'

'An—act?'

'Of course,' he said, and, taking pity on her wide-eyed and mystified expression, he explained, 'I'd finished my business in the study with her when she asked me not to make a fool of her in front of her friends. She asked if I'd leave it to her to tell them that she and I were no longer engaged.'

'Which you did?' Whitney questioned, realising as she spoke, that he must have done.

'As I said, I was tired,' he replied. 'I was weary and more interested in my bed than in being bothered what tale she told them about the broken engagement. I agreed to say nothing, provided that she emptied my home of unwanted guests straight away.'

'But she didn't empty...' her voice trailed off.

'She did not,' Sloan agreed. 'I was tired enough to sleep on the proverbial clothes-line, and went up to bed and don't even remember getting undressed. I certainly hadn't the remotest idea that one small portion of my bed was already occupied,' he said gently.

'I'm—sorry,' Whitney mumbled, and looked away from him while she collected herself together again, because really Sloan had so much charm that she felt quite without strength.

'There's no need to be,' he said softly, but, observing that she was not ready to look at him again yet, he resumed, 'I think I was as staggered as you when, having fallen asleep as soon as my head touched the pillow, I was rudely awakened by my ex-fiancée going into dramatics about how she'd trusted me. She'd asked me to leave it to her to announce to her friends that we were no longer engaged. That was her way of doing it.'

'Saving her face by leaving you as the guilty party!' Whitney caught on.

'And leaving me, if I wanted any rest at all that night, to get rid of that crowd myself,' he completed.

'Is that where you went when you left the bedroom—to get Gleda's guests off your premises?' Whitney gasped. 'I thought you'd gone to make it up with her!'

'I'd had it with her, and with all her half-stoned friends. I wanted my home to myself.'

'But you didn't have it to yourself. I got left behind and...'

'You got left behind, and I,' he said, 'I was subsequently turned into a liar.'

'Oh!' Whitney breathed. But as her brain started to wake up, she exclaimed angrily, 'Urgh!' realising that, without her knowing it, he'd had her believing every word he'd said. 'I must be the most gullible female who ever lived! I *believed* you!' she stormed. 'Knowing damn well how you've lied to me, I *actually* believed that load of rubbish you've just fed me!' Fuming, she would have jerked to her feet, but Sloan was swift to stretch out his hands to her arms and to hold her still.

'It wasn't rubbish, Whitney, it was the truth,' he told her as she tried, unsuccessfully, to knock his hands from her arms. 'Believe me, every word that I've told you since I entered your flat today has been the truth.' Speaking quickly, the sooner to get her calmed down, he swiftly added, 'It was only after I met you that—that, without comprehending why initially, I found that for the first time in my life, I was hiding behind lies.'

Realising that she was fighting a losing battle in trying to get free from hands which just weren't going to release her until she was quieted, Whitney sank a little further back in her chair and tried again for calm. To her relief, Sloan let go his hold on her.

'Supposing—just supposing,' she pushed out from between stiff and hostile lips, 'that I believe, as you've said, that your engagement was broken before you came home that night. Why, if it wasn't for purposes of revenge, did you phone me at my office some weeks later? Why, knowing I'd only agreed to dine with you that night because I wanted to help in any way I could, did you then fill me up with that dreadful story of your mother's accident?'

'I spent the two weeks following our first dinner date wondering the same thing myself,' Sloan admitted, and sent her heartbeats into rapid acceleration when he revealed, 'Prior to our first date, I'd gone through almost three weeks with the memory of you insisting on intruding on my every day. At the end of those three weeks, when according to my way of thinking you should have been completely out of my head—but weren't—I thought I'd better take another look at you.'

'You make it sound like some clinical exercise!' Whitney denied her fast-beating heart to tell him tartly.

'It was never that,' Sloan murmured, and made her heart pound with renewed vigour when he went on, 'I soon realised that my only motive for asking you out was that, purely and simply, I wanted to see you again.'

Her throat felt so choked that it was a wonder to Whitney that her voice should come out so clearly when, as if only marginally interested, she said, 'Is that so?'

Sloan nodded, as he told her, 'I was brought down to earth with a resounding crash when you suddenly showed that your reasons for sharing dinner with me that night were nothing to do with any reciprocal feeling that you wanted to see me again, too.'

'Set you back on your heels, did it?' she asked him acidly, while wishing that her giddy heart would behave as sensibly as her head, which just knew, most definitely, that this was the longest garden path she had ever had the misfortune to be led up. 'Naturally I see now that you were being nothing but honest when you told me that night that you and Gleda would never marry,' she went on witheringly. 'Naturally, too,' she snapped, as she recalled some of their discussion that night, 'having seen that I am—was—a little sensitive when it comes to a mother's suffering, you just couldn't resist making up the story you did about your mother.'

'I can't deny it,' Sloan replied. 'Though if it's of any help, I went through the next two weeks being stunned at the liar you had made of me.'

'Well, I just knew it would end up being all my fault!' Whitney flared.

'Who else should I blame?' he asked, unnerving her by taking hold of her hands in her lap, and looking steadily into her eyes. 'Through you, pride and the instinct to keep my head down have seen me lie when never in my life have I lied, or found the need to weave such blatant falsehoods to any female.'

'That's the sort of back-handed compliment I adore,' Whitney told him faintly, the sour note she had searched for not to be found anywhere.

She tried to snatch her hands from his grasp, but he would not let them go. Then suddenly she was not sure if it was he who was gripping her hands, or she who gripped his, when all at once he confessed, 'You've got me so all over the place, Whitney Lawford, that it doesn't surprise me that I'm getting it all wrong and don't know what the hell I'm doing or saying.'

She knew the feeling, it applied to *her*, but surely not to him! Staring at him, she tried desperately hard for something brittle, or sarcastic, or for anything at all which would conceal the fact that she was starting to fall apart at the seams. But her voice was not sarcastic, brittle or hard when all she managed to say was a choky-sounding, 'It—er—sounds painful.'

'It is, believe me, it is,' he told her, and seemed about to go on, when he hesitated. Not too long ago she had been quite positive that she would never again believe another word he said. Yet, when she well knew that he could be hesitating while he thought up fresh lies, the most idiotic idea dropped into her head that he was hesitating because, for some reason, he was unsure of himself! But, even knowing just how idiotic her idea was—because she had never met a man who was so colossally confident over just about everything—Whitney found she was still waiting and still ready to listen when, taking a steadying breath, Sloan continued, 'It seems, now, that I've been in a perpetual state of alternating happiness, anguish and apprehension since the first time I met you, my dear.'

Desperately, she sought for some trite or stinging comment. But, as he had described many of her own feelings since she had met him, all she could murmur was, 'You—er—have?'

'I was irritable at first,' he went on, 'and with just cause, since I'd come home to find that my house had been invaded. But, after catching up on some missed sleep, I came downstairs to find you asleep on my couch.'

'I—remember,' she said jerkily, and at the tender smile that came to his mouth at her jerky tone, Whitney remembered too how breathless she had felt that morning when Sloan had reached down to that couch to haul her to her feet.

That same feeling of breathlessness returned when he said softly, 'I looked down at your gentle, sleeping expression and knew then that something was happening to me.'

'You—did?' In the grip of she knew not what, any feeling that he might be lying to her was gone as Whitney looked into the sincere grey of his eyes. 'Er—what was it? Did you know?' she asked from a dry throat.

'I didn't know then,' he replied. 'All I knew was that some alien force was at work, urging me to go and fetch a blanket to make sure that you weren't cold.'

'Oh,' she said, and swallowed. 'But—you didn't fetch a blanket.'

'I was about to when you stirred and opened your eyes. And, yes,' he went on, 'your eyes really were the fabulous green I thought I had dreamed, and I knew then that I wanted to get to know you better.'

Suddenly, Whitney lost her feeling of being mesmerised. 'It didn't sound like it!' she retorted shortly. 'From what I recall, no sooner had I got my eyes open than you were biting my head off.'

'If you recall that, Whitney,' he said mildly, strangely, not rising to her sharp tone, 'then you'll also recall that no sooner had you opened your eyes than, when I was half-way to planning to spend the day with you, all you could think of was to get away from me. All you wanted to do was to get back to this flat.'

'I . . .' she said, and had no defence, although she was not altogether sure why she should think she needed one. But Sloan was going on.

'Can you wonder that after such treatment I should stand out against contacting you?'

'But you did contact me! You rang . . .'

'I folded completely,' he owned, 'when twenty days later you were still in my head.'

'I . . . You . . .' Whitney tried again. 'You really did want to see me for—me! I mean,' she hurried on when that sounded double Dutch to her, though that didn't totally surprise her, 'I thought you only wanted to see me because—er—so that I could try and help with your broken engagement. Ah!' she said, and even though she felt that she was talking nineteen to the dozen, she was suddenly beset by nerves, by shock and by emotions which she could not put a name to, for she could not stop the words bubbling from her. 'But you'd already broken your engagement—you, I mean, not Gleda—so you couldn't have wanted your engagement mended anyway. So...' Whitney slowed down and brought out the only thing that her intelligence had left her with '... you must have wanted to go out with me...' Abruptly, she broke off, then shock and nerves and everything else was leaving her, because he just had to be leading her up the garden path. 'You *rat*!' she hurled at him, yanking her hands out of his unsuspecting clasp. 'You lying, treacherous swine!' she berated him, while Sloan, blocking any chance she had of getting to her feet, stared in astonishment at this sudden change in her. 'Of course you wanted to see me!' she raged. 'And naturally, you always fill up the females you want to see with all that guff about your mother!' she stormed.

'No, I don't' Sloan replied angrily. 'You're the only...'

'Oh, I get it!' Whitney flared hostilely. 'I'm special, am I? I'm the...'

'Yes, you are, damn you!' Sloan shouted. 'You're so special to me that, as I told you, I don't know where the hell I am any more.'

'Well, I...!' Again determined that she was not going to listen to another lying word, Sloan's reply only then sank in. Her voice was much less angry when, nervous again, she tried for a cool note, to say offhandedly, 'Really?'

'Really!' Sloan confirmed, his tone cool too, though a warmth began to creep in as he went on, 'What in thunder was I supposed to do? There was I out to dinner with a female whose company I was enjoying, whose beauty I admired, and whose conversation, sense of humour, her whole being, had me more and more fascinated as the evening wore on. But a female, I was made to realise as our dinner date drew to a close, who had not accepted my invitation from any feeling that she would like to see me again too, but, far from being interested in me, was trying to get me back with some other woman.'

Put like that, it didn't sound very flattering to him, Whitney had to admit. 'You could hardly blame me for that, though,' she bounced back, having more than enough to be going on with that Sloan had said he had admired her beauty and had enjoyed her company. 'According to what I believed—and you hadn't told me differently——' she accused, 'I was the reason for your engagement being broken in the first place. And,' her brain woke up to prod, 'whether you wanted to keep the truth of who ended your engagement to yourself or not, and regardless of my—er—indifference—to you...' she faltered, biting off the words she so nearly had added—'at the time'—and hardened her heart when she saw something that looked like a flicker of pain cross his features at her statement that she was indifferent to him. 'What possible reason—if we rule out revenge—can you have for lying, and for keeping on lying, about your mother?' she resumed to challenge.

'Pride,' Sloan replied straight away. 'Pride, I think, made me tell that first lie from which all else followed. Pride not to let you know that it rankled that you weren't dining with me out of any wish to spend some time in my company. You'd made that very plain.'

'Oh,' Whitney murmured softly, finding that her heart was nowhere as hard as she would have liked it to be.

'I'd definitely decided that if you felt like that then, devil take you, I wasn't going to ring you again.'

'Was that why you sounded so disagreeable when you rang me at the office and ordered me to give you my home telephone number?' Whitney asked, and was full of love for him when he nodded.

'I'm sorry,' he apologised. 'I'd just given in after two weeks of being determined not to. Pride was joined by instincts of self-preservation when, having made use of your home number in vain, I was assaulted by enraged feelings of jealousy when I rang the next night, only to have you tell me that the reason you hadn't answered your phone the night before was because you were out with some other man.'

'You—were jealous?' Whitney asked, her heart starting to beat so violently that she could hardly breathe.

'I've been almost insane with it,' Sloan confessed. 'Even when my instincts of self-preservation refused to allow me to see why I was so jealous, I wanted to make sure that you dated no one else but me.'

'Oh—Sloan!' Whitney gasped on a whisper, and, even while she was aware that there was still some explaining to be done, she just could not hold back from asking, albeit haltingly, 'What—is it that—you're saying?'

For long, endless moments Sloan sat and looked deeply into her eyes. 'I'm saying,' he began then, 'that, while I've been too proud to let you see how it mattered to me that you didn't care whether you went out with me or not, I haven't been too proud to lie to you. I'm saying,' he continued, 'that fear that you would refuse to go out with me again saw me perpetuating that lie.' Sloan's eyes were still fixed on hers when, as if to gain strength from some physical contact with her, he reached for her hands. He was holding them in his large, warm clasp when, very quietly, he told her, 'I'm saying, simply, my dear, dear Whitney, that—I love you.'

'Oh . . . !' she sighed on a gossamer breath, and she swallowed hard. 'You wouldn't . . .' she began to ask on a broken, husky note, '. . . lie to me, over a th-thing like that, would you?'

'It means something to you, then!' he exclaimed in some urgency. 'My loving you means something...' Suddenly he checked. 'I'm sorry,' he apologised. 'I've said you've got me all over the place, and it's true.' He then seemed to think that he had not earned the right to know how she felt until he had convinced her of his own feelings, for, holding her hands more firmly in his grip, he implored, 'Trust me, Whitney, please try to trust me! I know I've done nothing but give you cause not to believe a word I say, but if you believe nothing else— believe that I love you with everything that's in me.'

There was no mistaking his sincerity, and Whitney felt as if her heart would burst. A great and overwhelming joy broke in her, and she not only wanted to trust him, but every instinct within her told her she should.

'Oh, Sloan,' she said shakily, 'I don't know what— to say.'

Looking seriously into her wide and shining green eyes, Sloan took a yet firmer hold on her hands. 'You could try, for a start,' he said throatily, 'telling me that you don't—hate me.'

'I don't hate you,' she whispered.

'You could tell me that you—like me a little,' he instructed.

'I like you—a lot,' Whitney told him.

'You could tell me,' he said, and Whitney actually saw him take something of a nervous swallow before he went on, 'that you—love me—just a very little—perhaps?'

'Oh, Sloan,' Whitney cried, and she was so emotionally moved just then that she was very close to tears, 'I love you, with all that's in me.'

What she expected to happen then, she could not have said, but she had not expected that Sloan should tighten his grip on her fingers, and should challenge her hoarsely, 'You—wouldn't lie to me—to get your own back?'

Bravely she withstood the bruising pressure of his grip on her hands, and in the taut silence that followed she could read the torment in his eyes as he waited for her answer.

'I would never lie to any man over a thing like that,' she quickly told him, and, using the words he had used on her, she was suddenly made even more aware of how sincerely he had meant them, when *she* sincerely pleaded, 'Trust me, Sloan.'

Perhaps two more seconds elapsed, with Sloan crushing the fingers that lay in his hold, though saying nothing. Then, 'Oh, my love, my life!' he cried, and somehow—Whitney never quite knew how it was achieved—the hands that had been threatening to fracture hers had suddenly lifted her. And in one movement, or so it seemed, he had moved her so that the next she knew was that she was on his lap in his chair and he was holding her tightly up against his heart.

Minute after minute ticked by while Sloan alternately held her and put her from him to look into her face. 'When?' he asked. 'When did you know?'

'I knew that night you first kissed me,' Whitney, her trust in Sloan growing in leaps and bounds, replied openly.

'That night!' he exclaimed incredulously. 'But I'd been a swine that night!'

'It—er—had been a pretty disastrous evening,' she understated softly, and was in seventh heaven when Sloan's fabulous grin came out.

'That's putting it mildly,' he murmured. 'But it was all my fault,' he shouldered the blame. 'I'd broken all records to get my work in Switzerland done so I could get back to you,' he recalled. 'But when I phoned you, what do you do but tell me you've a date with Keston? Then, in the restaurant, while I'm still not over my jealousy about him, lo and behold, you ex-lover, Selby, walks in.'

'He was never my lover!' Whitney said quickly. 'Well, not in the accepted use of the word.'

'I know that now, my love,' Sloan said tenderly, 'but I didn't know it then. You'd spoken some time previously of having found out too late that he was married, and I just assumed you meant you'd been lovers.'

'I meant only that I'd fallen for him, not knowing he was married,' Whitney told him quickly. 'But in actual fact, I didn't know at all what it felt like to fall in love, until...' her voice started to fade '...until I met you,' she ended huskily.

'My sweet love,' Sloan breathed, and all was quiet in the room for some minutes when, holding her close, he traced kisses over her face, with his lips at last coming to rest over hers.

But soon he wanted to look into her face again, and as their kiss broke, time passed while content in each other's arms, they gazed at each other.

'When did you?' Whitney asked.

'Know that I was in love with you?' Sloan asked, so much on her wavelength now that he was able to pick up easily what she was asking. 'I'd known for some time, but in view of my recent escape from one engagement, I was suspicious of anything with a "love" label on it. But I, too, my dear,' he told her, 'was soon to discover that I didn't know what it was like to fall in love—until I met you.'

'You didn't truly love Gleda?'

'Now that I know what real love feels like, I can wholeheartedly say that I was never remotely in love with her. My love for you, now,' he went on, 'had me hiding behind a barrier of self-preservation. But that barrier started to crumble for me on the night that I kissed you and found out for myself that you weren't in love with Selby.'

'You knew that you loved me—that same night!'

'I think I knew before then, but I wasn't ready to accept it. In actual fact, it took me from that Saturday night to the following Friday night to face the knowledge that I was utterly and completely in love with you. And also,' he went on, 'to face the fact that you were going to play hell when I told you of my deception with regard to my mother's accident.'

'You—intended to tell me?'

'Of course,' Sloan replied stoutly. 'By Saturday morning, though, I was in quite a state.'

'You were?'

Sloan nodded as he told her, 'Part of me was clinging hard on to the memory of how you'd reacted—er— favourably to my kisses, and how, one particular dinner date excluded, we'd seemed to be happy in each other's company on most occasions. Could it be, I started to hope, that maybe you'd learned to care in some small way for me?'

'What did you decide?' Whitney asked him softly.

'My head was so full of doubts and fears that I couldn't come to any conclusion which wasn't hit on the head by some other thought a minute later,' he owned. 'So that in the end all I knew for sure was that I must confess everything to you, and see how things went from there.'

'Ah,' said Whitney as some light started to dawn. 'Was that why you invited me to dine at Heathlands that Saturday night?'

'It was,' he agreed. 'Bearing in mind that the last time I'd been in your flat, your neighbour had come banging on the door, regardless of the hour, I decided to get you where I stood no chance of being interrupted.'

'Fortunately, your housekeeper had the night off,' Whitney took up.

'I gave her the night off,' he told her, 'and dropped her off at her daughter's on my way to collect you.'

'You were very quiet on the way down,' Whitney recalled.

'I had a lot on my mind,' Sloan admitted, and just could not resist saluting her mouth with a loving kiss. 'I was fully determined to tell you everything,' he resumed when, their kiss broken, some seconds had elapsed while he regained his thread. 'But I became more and more enchanted by you as the evening wore on, and I discovered in myself a mighty aversion to confessing anything and so ruining what was turning out to be a perfect evening. Then all too soon you were talking of washing up and of going home, and I knew I could delay no longer.'

'But you did,' Whitney said gently, sensitive to him now, and able to see how it had been.

'I didn't mean to,' he revealed. 'I still needed you in my home, from where you couldn't easily run away, when I told you. I still didn't want any interruptions when once I began. And that,' he said, 'is the only reason why I agreed to you doing the washing up. I was about to start confessing everything,' he went on, but he had no need to finish.

'When I dropped that dish and got soaked,' Whitney finished for him.

Gently he kissed her. 'You know the rest, sweet love,' he whispered. 'I know I was wrong to make love to you before I'd explained everything. But the situation was upon me before I could think, and, oh, my love, to have you in my arms sent every sane and logical thought out of my head. I loved you, was in love with you, and, dared I believe it, it felt as if you loved me a little too. I'm not super-human, darling.'

Gently, Whitney reached up and kissed him, for it seemed to her then that, if she had been in an agony of mind since she had last seen him, Sloan had also known that same agony.

'Forgive me?' he asked softly.

'You know I do,' she whispered, but she just had to ask, 'Why, Sloan, did you leave me to wake up in that big bed alone?'

'Oh, my dear, I've hurt you so much...' He broke off, but he quickly resumed to tell her, 'I never meant that you should know a moment's hurt that day. We'd made love at dawn and I was certain that to have given of yourself the way you had must mean that you cared for me. You had fallen asleep again,' he told her, 'and you looked every bit as beautiful asleep as you do awake. I stayed looking at your dear face for some minutes and felt almost compelled to wake you and tell you I loved you.'

'Oh, how I wish that you had,' Whitney whispered.

'No more than I,' Sloan breathed, and he looked adoringly down at her. 'But in my love for you, I found a new sort of caring,' he went on. 'I wanted to wake you, but something held me back. Through me, through our lovemaking, you were exhausted. I determined then that you must rest and, certain that you wouldn't wake for hours, I then had the insane idea to go looking for a perfect red rose.'

'A—red rose?' Whitney queried.

'Dammit,' Sloan breathed, 'I'd never felt like that before. I wanted you to wake and find a red rose on the pillow next to you. I wanted to be there when you turned your head and saw the rose. I wanted to be there to see if you would smile that warm dream of a smile you had smiled earlier. And, if smile you did, I wanted to be there to tell you of my love and to ask you to marry me.'

'You were going to... Oh, my poor Sloan!' Whitney cried, realisation hitting her right then that she must have hurt him just as much as he had hurt her.

'It's all right,' he shushed her. 'Everything's all right now.'

'But I hurt you,' she said contritely.

'As I deserved to be hurt,' he accepted, and, after telling her that it had taken him longer than he'd anticipated in tracking down a perfect red rose on that early Sunday morning, he went on, 'Though I was more totally crushed than merely hurt when, tiptoeing into my room with my booty, I found not only that you were gone, but there, on the pillow where I'd been all set to place the rose, was the message you had left.'

'Oh, how can you ever forgive me?' Whitney wailed in some torment.

'Easily, my love,' Sloan quickly assured her, and kissed her, and told her how he had sprinted to his car and had started to chase after her.

'But you changed your mind?'

'I hadn't got very far when I realised that I'd better pull over, and think it all out. It was then that I was hit by a sensitivity that I didn't know I had, and I began to be besieged by the fear that if I went chasing after you, you'd reject me outright. I'd thought,' he smiled tenderly, 'that you must have cared something for me to have given yourself the way you had. But to have written that you'd never forgive me, *ever*, seemed to me to be all the proof I needed that you not only did *not* care for me but that you blamed me entirely for what had happened and were now bitterly regretting having given yourself to me.'

'I might have been regretting it then,' Whitney told him softly, 'but only because of what Mrs Orton had told me. I gave myself to you willingly, and in love,' she told him shyly.

'Sweet Whitney,' he breathed, and placed featherlight kisses on her eyes. 'God knows where I went for the rest of that day, for I've no idea,' he resumed as if, now that they were talking, she must know everything. 'All I knew was that when you had to be mine, you just did not want to know. I then sent you the painting which you'd liked so much—hoping to establish some point of contact—and knew the depths of despair when it came back with its own message.'

'I'm so sorry,' Whitney murmured, and just had to ask, 'Your note said that you'd bought that picture some time ago, but...?'

'It was no lie, my love,' he told her. 'I purchased the picture the day after I'd looked down into your excited, shining green eyes in that gallery. It was the first time in my life that I was conscious of my heart actually starting to thud.'

'Honestly?' she asked, but she was not really doubting his word.

'Honestly,' he replied. 'I think I was in love with you then, but wasn't prepared to admit it.' Whitney smiled happily, and he went on, 'Anyhow, I returned to the gallery and bought the painting and was just going to give them your address for delivery, when suddenly I got cold feet.'

'You—cold feet?' Whitney teased.

'Hell,' Sloan grinned at her teasing, 'I'd just extracted myself from one engagement; I wasn't ready to get involved again.

'But you are ready now?'

'You've made me sweat long enough, young woman,' he told her mock-severely. 'You can have no idea of the many times I reached for the phone to ring you when that picture came back.'

'But you didn't ring.'

'I couldn't, not then,' he said. 'I just couldn't bear to have the words "I hate you" added to that "I'll never forgive you". Then, everything blew up on the business I was setting up abroad, and I had to jet off to sort it all out. And only when that was settled did I have the chance to take a long look at my life, my present unhappiness. I just knew, Whitney, that I couldn't take another month like the last one. I decided that I'd have to do something about it.'

'So you decided to phone me when you were back in England,' Whitney documented, loving the comfort his strong-muscled arms afforded.

'I decided to phone you,' Sloan agreed. 'Though first, and bearing in mind that you had shown a marked sensitivity with regard to my mother, I put through a call to her on her cruise ship and told her that I needed her most urgently at Heathlands.'

'W-what?' Whitney gasped. 'W-why?' she spluttered.

'I needed to have some reason to contact you. A reason which, if everything went well, wouldn't see you put the phone down on me the second you knew who it was. I had it all rehearsed, what I would say,' Sloan went on. 'And as soon as my mother and her husband had flown in and had arrived at my home, then with the words, "My mother is at Heathlands and particularly wants to see you" on the tip of my tongue, I dialled your number.' Whitney's eyes were saucer-wide as he continued, 'But no sooner did I hear your much yearned-for, much missed, and heart-palpitation-making voice than I forgot every word of what I had rehearsed. Instead I found that I was asking a question which was more important to me: whether you had forgiven me yet. Your reply, my true love, knocked me for six.'

'You—er—must have driven like a demon to have got here so quickly,' Whitney breathed.

'Possibly,' he conceded. 'I don't remember much of the drive. You'd used the word "unwanted" about our baby, and I must have been half crazy, but all I could think of was that you might be thinking of having an abortion and that I had to get to you fast or my one faint chance of getting you to marry me might be gone.'

'Oh, Sloan,' Whitney cried, and she felt emotional tears stinging her eyes again. 'But you don't have to marry me,' she thought she should tell him. To her delight, she was swiftly made to see that any such suggestion was mightily frowned upon.

'Oh, for God's sake, don't start giving me nightmares at this stage!' he told her forcefully. 'Just promise me, Whitney, that you'll marry me as soon as I can arrange it for one day next week. Promise me,' he insisted, when she did not answer him quickly enough.

'If you put it like that,' she responded. 'Though I have to tell you that once my word is given, I never break a promise.'

'Say after me,' Sloan instructed, 'I promise...'

'I promise,' Whitney obliged.

'That I...'

'That I,' she repeated.

'Will marry Sloan Illingworth...'

'Will marry Sloan Illingworth.'

'As soon as it can be arranged.'

'As soon as it can be arranged,' she complied, and smiled, simply because Sloan smiled.

'Now kiss me,' he further ordered.

'I hope you're not going to be as bossy as this when we're married,' Whitney returned cheerfully.

'I'll be putty in your hands, and you know it,' Sloan murmured, and claimed her lips.

This is an advertisement for Book Mate · I.